DARLING
GIRL

DARLING GIRL

TERRY H. WATKINS

GREEN PLACE BOOKS *Brattleboro, Vermont*

Printed in the United States

10 9 8 7 6 5 4 3 2 1

Green Writers Press is a Vermont-based publisher whose mission is to spread
a message of hope and renewal through the words and images we publish.
Throughout we will adhere to our commitment to preserving and protecting
the natural resources of the earth. To that end, a percentage of our proceeds
will be donated to environmental activist groups and The Southern Poverty
Law Foundation. Green Writers Press gratefully acknowledges support from
individual donors, friends, and readers to help support the environment
and our publishing initiative. Green Place Books curates books that tell
literary and compelling stories with a focus on writing about place—these
books are more personal stories/memoir and biographies.

GREEN
PLACE
BOOKS

GReen
writers
press

Giving Voice to Writers & Artists Who Will Make the World a Better Place
Green Writers Press | Brattleboro, Vermont
www.greenwriterspress.com

ISBN: 978-1-7322662-4-7

PRINTED ON PAPER WITH PULP THAT COMES FROM FSC (FOREST STEWARDSHIP COUNCIL)-CERTIFIED, MANAGED
FORESTS THAT GUARANTEE RESPONSIBLE ENVIRONMENTAL, SOCIAL, AND ECONOMIC PRACTICES BY LIGHTNING
SOURCE. ALL WOOD-PRODUCT COMPONENTS USED IN BLACK & WHITE OR STANDARD COLOR PAPERBACK BOOKS,
UTILIZING EITHER CREAM OR WHITE BOOKBLOCK PAPER, THAT ARE MANUFACTURED IN THE LAVERGNE,
TENNESSEE, PRODUCTION CENTER ARE SUSTAINABLE FORESTRY INITIATIVE® (SFI®) CERTIFIED SOURCING.

DARLING GIRL

CHAPTER ONE

⊰ ⊱

1957 — Gone

I AM FIVE YEARS OLD the first time my mama goes away.
Gramma stands in my mama's place outside Immaculate
Conception, squinting in the summer sunlight. She's got
the baby, Samuel Taylor, on one hip, and my other brother,
Henry David, hangs off her right arm.

"Where's my mama?" I ask her. "Are we getting another
baby? We really need a girl this time!"

Gramma doesn't answer, just gets that look all my
grownups get sometimes. She turns and nods toward the
black Desoto with the sweeping fins, parked partway up
on the curb. My daddy says Grampa doesn't know to stop
unless he runs into something. You can hardly see Grampa's
head over the steering wheel.

I love Grampa's car. He calls it Liz, or sometimes Titsloren, which makes my mama punch him on the arm and say, "Not in front of her," which means me. The car gleams, because he washes it every day and shoe-polishes the whitewalls. Inside, it's red—my favorite color, even if it does clash with my red hair, which isn't really red, more orange. I need to ask Grampa what *whorehouse* means, because that's what my daddy says whenever he sees that car. I think maybe Grampa will let me drive, so I run around to his window and lean in. He's already scooting back the seat just enough to squeeze me in.

Gramma puts the baby in the port-a-crib in the back seat. Henry David crawls up on the window ledge in back to stretch out. I can't believe he rides like that even when it's this hot, but you can't tell him anything. Gramma gets in and slams the door a little harder than you really have to to get it to close. Grampa looks at her over the rims of his little round sunglasses but just says, "Olivia," in his *don't* voice. Grampa's car doesn't have a regular PRNDL handle, so I push the D button, and off we go.

Grampa gives directions and works the pedals since I can't reach, but I do all the really hard work, like steering and staying inside the lines and ducking when the deputy rolls by in his patrol car. I tell Grampa when to slow down or go fast—which I don't, hardly ever—and when he needs to start braking. He says, "Good girl!" when I get it right and "Are you sure?" when I don't, and he never, ever yells at me. Sweat rolls down the backs of my legs from the bend in my knees, but there's a breeze through the open windows, so it's not really like an oven like Gramma says.

We turn right at the last corner, which means we're going to the Tastee Freez instead of straight home. Now I'm sure it's a new baby, because we always go the Tastee Freez when they're picking out a new baby. I can't wait to tell my daddy when he gets home. We get out of the Desoto to eat our ice cream, because nobody ever eats anything in Grampa's car. He asks me about vacation Bible school. Me and Grampa wonder if the sisters don't get real hot in their getups. I think they should at least have short-sleeved ones for summer, or maybe some other color instead of black, and Grampa says I ought to tell Mother Superior that. Gramma spills her ice cream on the baby, which makes him cry, and she says, "Good heavens, Edwin!" and then it's time to go. I let Grampa drive by himself this time so I can sit in the back and hang my head out the window to catch the breeze.

Gramma and Grampa are fussing in the front seat, which is something they always do when they think nobody's listening. I'm always listening, even when I'm not supposed to be. They are talking about "someplace nice," "getting help," and "*he's* her problem"—stuff that doesn't make any sense, but that I save for when it will. Gramma keeps looking back to make sure I'm not paying attention, and I keep looking out the car window.

At Gramma's house, Grampa's already set up the wading pool, and after he scoops out the drowned ants, me and Henry David strip down to our underpants and splash all the water out quick as we can. Grampa chases us around the yard with the hose, threatening all kinds of stuff we know he'll never do. After he refills the pool, Grampa pulls up his lawn chair, putting his feet in the pool and the baby between his feet. We all mostly just loll around. We're careful not to get Samuel Taylor's face wet, or he'll cry, and that'll just bring Gramma down on us and then we'll all have to take a nap.

Mostly, I'm hoping that Gramma brought my new dress to wear to the hospital and all the petticoats that go with it, and that she remembered to bring ties for the boys, even if she thinks it's silly to put ties on little boys. My daddy's real particular about how we look when we go out with him, and I don't ever want to disappoint my daddy.

When I'm all pruned up, I ask Grampa, "When are we going?"

"Going where?" he replies in his not-really-paying-attention voice, twisting Samuel Taylor's wet hair into curls.

"To the hospital, Grampa!" Sometimes, you gotta remind him about stuff, because his mind just wanders off. Grampa scoops up the baby and scoots real fast across the yard, hollering "Olivia!" in his come-here-right-now voice. Gramma opens the screen door, wipes her hands on her apron, and says it's time for a nap and she can't believe he let us run around out there half-naked for the whole world to see.

Gramma drags me inside and stands me up on the toilet seat lid to brush and re-braid my hair while Grampa puts the boys down. She's not real careful about the tangles like my mama is. But Gramma's much better at keeping up with things than Grampa, so I ask her, "When are we going to the hospital?"

Gramma stops braiding for just a minute, and it gets real quiet. She says, "We're not going to any hospital."

"But who's gonna pick out the new baby? If we let my daddy do it, he'll just get us another boy."

"Good heavens! The things you say! The last thing your mother needs is another baby! That's not where your father is." She's braiding my hair real tight now and jerking my head back a little while she does, but she doesn't mean to. Gramma's just excitable.

"Well, where are they then? We didn't get the map out. We always get the map out." They go away a lot, my mama and my daddy. We always get the map out so I know where they'll be, and can worry about the right stuff—like alligators if it's Florida, or avalanches if it's Minnesota, or earthquakes if it's California, or seat cushions that float if it's Havana. And I still worry about that one all the time, because not one of the chair cushions I put in the pool ever floated, not even for a minute.

Gramma turns me around to face her and tucks some short stray hairs behind my ears where I cut bangs when I shouldn't have. I cut Henry David's hair, too, but nobody seems to care that somebody's hair *has* to get cut when you're playing Beauty Parlor. Hair just grows right back anyway. Now, even the fingernail scissors stay in the drawer unless I have a really good reason, like paper dolls and a grownup who's looking right at me when they say it's okay.

Gramma's looking right at me now, and I start worrying that there's something else, something new I did that I need to have a good excuse about in case she asks. Finally, she says, "Your father will be home for dinner. He hasn't gone any-where." Well, that's good because I'm all out of excuses for stuff I've done, but now my mind is racing around for the right question: the one she'll answer.

Everybody always says I just blurt out whatever I'm think-ing, but that's not true. I think lots of stuff nobody knows about, like how come I don't stutter in my head, and how will we know if Henry David stutters, too, if he doesn't ever talk, and why the boys all have two names and I don't even have one. I'm real careful about what I say on account of some-times it makes my mama cry, and where is my mama? She never goes anywhere alone. I don't even think I've ever seen my mama alone. If I ask that, will Gramma answer?

She's already moving down the hall, saying, "Let's look at pictures," which is just about my favorite thing to do in the whole world, so I don't ask. Dead relatives and Gramma as a flapper fill cardboard boxes kept under the bed.

Later, Gramma plays the piano, and we sing "Dead in the Coach Ahead" and "I'm Only a Bird in a Gilded Cage." Grampa, who doesn't sing, recites a poem, "Little Willie," and Gramma says "Oh, Ned," in her aggravated voice, which is practically her only voice. We have wienies and macaroni and cheese for dinner because that's Henry David's favorite, but my daddy still doesn't come home, and then it's time for bed.

They put us down in the back bedroom, the one that's really mine, since I stay there when I come on vacation, which is different from just coming over to spend the night. Henry David is nearest the wall, Samuel Taylor in the middle so he won't roll off and break like our cousin Amy did, and me on the outside, because sometimes I get up in the middle of the night to make sure everything's all right. The boys go to sleep right away, but I stay awake listening for my daddy's car and hearing crickets and neighbors laughing and music far away....

...And loud voices in the front room. I must have fallen asleep, and it's probably real late. I can't tell who Gramma's yelling at, so after I check to make sure the boys are still breathing, I crawl out of bed and tiptoe down the long hall toward the front room. I wonder if the places where the floorboards meet are like cracks in the sidewalk, because I sure don't want to break anybody's back, especially not my mama's.

My daddy leans up against the wall, and Gramma's got her back up like a cat and she's hissing "...*your* fault..." at my daddy. I can tell she's winding up to give him a piece of her mind, so I better save him. I take a running jump at my daddy, and he catches me like always and swings me up high. I hug his neck and whisper "Daddy, Daddy, Daddy," right in his ear. He hugs me right back real tight, and I know everything is all right.

My daddy slides me around to his back and hooks his arms under my knees, and I rest my chin on his shoulder so I can see what's going on.

Gramma stands across the room, and I can tell she's real mad. Her mouth is a thin line, her eyes are hard and mean, she is vibrating like a guitar string, and it looks like her pin curls might just pop their metal clips at us.

"She should be in bed," Gramma spits out.

"You sleepy?" Daddy asks, and I shake my head "no" into his neck and hang on tight. "Let's go," says Daddy. Ignoring Gramma, he grabs an afghan off the sofa on his way out the door. She slams it hard behind us as we cross the yard.

In front of the house, my daddy tips me through his car window into the front seat, tossing the afghan over my head. It's dark and quiet out here. Me and my daddy are the only people awake in the whole world.

"Up or down?" he asks, and I say, "Down."

"You driving?" he asks, and I shake my head and say, "Not tonight."

He pushes a button and the soft top of the car slides away as we glide away from the curb into the night. I sit for a while with the afghan covering my feet because they're always cold, but as we leave town and head toward the highway, I stretch out across the front seat and lay my head in my daddy's lap. There's no crackle from the two-way radio like in the daytime, and the regular radio's playing real soft, far away rock 'n' roll on WLS out of Chicago, because all the radio stations around here go off the air at dark. My daddy has one hand on the steering wheel and the other on the top of my head. The end of his cigarette glows red in the dark.

"I can hear you thinking," he says. "You'll never fall asleep if you don't stop. Just watch the stars and go to sleep." I try, but it's real hard, and my head is so full of stuff tonight I probably got a question for every star I see flashing by.

"What'd you do to make Gramma so mad?"

"Your grandmother's always a little bit aggravated at me." And, boy, is that true! I don't think Gramma can stand my daddy. She's just about the only person who can't, because everybody else just loves him. Of course, I'm not sure Gramma can really stand anybody. But that's not what's bothering me tonight.

I'm quiet for a while, listening to the sound of the car on the road and the music on the radio, until finally I just blurt out, "Where's my mama? If we're not getting another baby, where'd she go?"

My daddy's hand reaches across me to turn off the radio. He flicks his cigarette out of the car, and after a while, says, "Your mama's real tired." Well, of course she's tired, it's the middle of the night. Only me and my daddy are ever up this time of night.

"Is she at our house?"

"No, your mama, she's gone away to rest—somewhere quiet." I think about all the noise me and the boys make, and I feel real bad. Except Henry David never makes any noise, and Samuel Taylor's just a baby, so the noise he makes doesn't count, and so it's all my fault, my fault, my fault.

"When's she coming back? She has to take me school shopping and bake cookies Friday for the end of vacation Bible school." There's lots of stuff only my mama does, and who's gonna take care of all that stuff if she's not here?

"Soon," he says, "She'll be back soon. Don't worry. We'll get your cookies. Go to sleep now. Go to sleep."

We drive on into the night, trees and stars and telephone wires flashing above us. My mama doesn't come home for a long time.

CHAPTER TWO

♧ ♧

1958 – Closet

IN HER CLOSET, it's pretty easy to imagine my mama is near. Dresses trail over my head as I crawl toward the back, careful not to disturb the stacked shoeboxes and wrapped handbags that tell me the story of her life. I can remember when and where she wore each dress, and which shoes and gloves and jewelry go together to make an outfit. I can still feel her here, in the perfume and in the brush of the dresses against my face. Everybody is saying nothing pretty loud, at least to me, and nobody cares that I miss her awful. My mama is gone again.

Mama fills up all kind of space when she's here. Down on the floor playing matchbox cars. Reciting *I Sweepa da Street* wearing a paper mustache and Grampa's baggy pants.

Singing "Detour, There's a Muddy Road Ahead" at the top of her lungs in the car with the top down and the boys in the port-a-crib in the back babbling along, but not Henry David, because he never talks. She takes up even more room when she's gone.

Gramma doesn't understand about Henry David, so she keeps trying to get him to ask for stuff, and he just sits there with those big eyes that say *sorry* and waits for her to give up. He's got all the patience in the world and never cries, just listens all the time. He understands everything. He's been to all kinds of doctors, and none of them make any difference. Sometimes, Mama and Daddy fight about him and say ugly things to each other. The last time we took him somewhere, the doctor said they ought to leave him there to live because they knew best how to take care of him and he wouldn't ever be right. My mama didn't say a word, just looked at that man like he was something nasty on her shoe, swooped up Henry David, and stormed out of there. My daddy unfolded from his chair, took my hand, said, "We're done here," wrote a check, and walked out. Mama held Henry David tight in her lap all the way home, even though he'd rather ride in the back window.

Most times, I can tell when he wants something. You just watch his face and hands real close. It's my job a lot to watch him, but he's not much trouble. He stays close, mostly does what you tell him, lets me read to him and never messes up my paper dolls. But boys can't play paper dolls forever, and when he goes to school, he's gonna have to talk—maybe not as much as me, but some. Other people don't understand and say those nasty-nice things like how he's so pretty he looks like a doll, and how it must be nice to have one child that doesn't make so much noise. Somebody's always saying,

"Bless his little heart," and how my mama must be a saint to put up with all this. Mama says to say, "Thank you" or "He's just fine," and not to kick the people who say mean things. Sometimes they make me want to spit.

But in the back of the closet, the stuff going on out there doesn't matter so much. If I especially like a dress, Mama draws it for my favorite paper doll, the one we glued to thick cardboard so she's really strong and doesn't get bent. She has the most clothes of all my paper dolls. She came with some, but the prettiest ones are the ones me and my mama make for her. I want to look like her when I grow up, with blonde hair that stays in place. My hair's too red, and both my grand-mothers complain that it won't stay braided and crawls out all over the place, no matter how tight they pull on it.

It's so hard to think about just one thing when there's so much happening that I don't understand. My head feels like it's full of bees. Willa Mae's daddy went away, and then she got a new one. I don't want a new mama, I want my same one back. I want to help her dress and watch her sweep down the stairs like Loretta Young.

Grampa's calling me and getting closer. It's funny, because he knocks on the closet door all serious and asks, "You in there?" When I tell him yes, he asks, "You coming out anytime soon?" I wonder what would happen if I said no, and just stayed in here until Mama comes back. I come out, though, because it's Grampa, and he is the safest place I know.

"Baseball game's on the radio. Want to come out and lis-ten? Cubs and Cardinals. I'm working on the car."

The baseball is always the Cubs and somebody, because Grampa grew up near Chicago. The car is real old, and he's been working on it in the shed behind the house my whole life. Grampa's workshop is kinda like Mama's closet—it tells you who he is. The smell of it and the things you find there are all a part of him. I know where he keeps all his tools, and I help him with the car. He's got it hooked up to a battery, and I sit in the front seat and listen to the ballgame. If he was gone, the shed is where I'd go to feel close to him.

"Who's winning?"

"Nobody yet. Scoreless in the third. Cubs still have a chance." Grampa always believes the Cubs still have a chance, no matter where they are in the standings. He says one day he'll take me to the World Series to watch the Cubs win it all.

He waits for me to crawl out of the closet, takes my hand, and pulls me up, not rushing, not yelling, just being. He grabs two Coca Colas on the way out through the kitchen.

"You thinking about your mama?"

"Yes, sir."

"You know your mama loves you and wouldn't go away if it wasn't for the best."

"Yes, sir. But why, Grampa? What's wrong with her?"

"Your mama, I think she just feels too much. Feels everything too much. Something that doesn't bother somebody else just breaks her, make her too sad to go on. Always did, even when she was a little girl," he says with a sigh.

"Will she get better?" I ask.

"She always gets better. It just doesn't last. It's like having a cold in the winter that you never quite get rid of. You feel better, stop taking your medicine, and it comes right back."

"Can we catch it from her, like you can a cold?" I think about last winter, when me and Henry David and Samuel Taylor all had a stomach bug at the same time. Mama put us all in the big bed in her room and made Daddy sleep on the couch. She slept across the foot of the bed while we threw up and cried. She told us stories and fed us soup, and pretty soon, we all felt better. I wonder if somebody keeps her company where she is and feeds her soup and rubs her back and tells her she'll feel better soon. I would do that for Mama, but when she feels bad enough, she always goes away.

Chapter Three

⊸ ⊶

1958 — Fourth of July

I<small>T'S THE</small> F<small>OURTH OF</small> J<small>ULY</small>, and everybody in town is staking out their territory in the park by the bandstand. Grampa likes to go real early and find the very best spot for watching the fireworks after dark, so we've been here since right after lunch. I bet he'd have spent the night here if Gramma would let him.

"The trick," he says, "is to figure out where the middle is."

Figuring it out takes all kind of measuring. First, he has to see where the firemen are setting up the display and what's on offer this year. I like the Catherine Wheels best. They look just like giant pinwheels on fire. Grampa loves them all. Once he knows where the setup is, he walks off some distances according to a plan he keeps in his head, and picks the perfect spot. We lay down our second-best quilts on the grass and settle in.

Gramma sits in a lawn chair crocheting an afghan. Gramma's house is knee-deep in afghans and antimacassars, all made by hand. She's been trying to teach me to crochet, but my hands are clumsy, and I have trouble keeping the instructions in my head. Grampa and Henry David have wandered off to shake and howdy with the other early birds, Grampa being more sociable than the rest of us. The baby, Samuel Taylor, is laying on quilts and telling a long story to a leaf he's picked up somewhere.

I always bring a book to read. Today, it is *Mrs. Wiggs of the Cabbage Patch*. It is hot, and I am full of ham and potato salad and a little drowsy. Later, Mama and Daddy will bring fried chicken and watermelon for supper. I wonder what they are doing right now. Mama has been awful tired since she got back from resting. Nobody wants to talk about it. Except at school, Buddy Ray said she went crazy and tried to hurt herself, so I drew a picture that made him look uglier than he already is and hung it on the chalkboard.

Soft voices and laughter float in the late-afternoon air. Critters are buzzing in the background, and birds dart here and there. A breeze ruffles my hair where it has escaped from the braids Mama and Gramma use to tame it. It's too hot to do much of anything except lay around, and that's what most people are doing. Some boys toss a ball, but without much energy. The band is warming up and tuning their instruments in the background, and their noise finally turns into a song I recognize.

Grampa strolls up to Gramma sitting in her lawn chair, makes a little bow, and holds out his hand. She shakes her head no but lets herself be coaxed to her feet anyway. Grampa sweeps her into his arms, and they begin to waltz a tight little circle in one corner on the second-best quilts. I watch as they dance and Grampa sings in a quiet voice, *"Casey would waltz with the strawberry blonde, and the band played on."*

Gramma's a little bit taller than Grampa, but you don't usually notice it. It doesn't show now as they dance because she rests her head lightly on his shoulder. Just for a minute, I see them as they are in the old pictures we look at, and as they must have been when Gramma was a strawberry blonde and rolled her stockings and rouged her knees, and Grampa wore a pork pie hat and a coonskin coat. Before Grampa's heart attacks and Gramma's anger. Before they were anybody's Gramma and Grampa.

When the music stops, she pushes him away and says, "Don't be silly, Ned!" Grampa just grins and lets her go. He strolls off on his rounds, still singing: *"...his brain was so loaded it nearly exploded, and the band played on."*

CHAPTER FOUR

❧ ❧

1958 — Moving Around

BECAUSE DADDY IS A PIPELINER, we move all the time. Before I started school, we moved every time the warehouse moved, which was as often as every three weeks. Pipelining is the most important job in the world, because you wouldn't have gas for your car or water or gas for heating and cooking, which is not the same kind of gas as gasoline without it. My daddy's job is the most important of all, because he's project manager. Whenever there's a war, my daddy works for the government, but not just in the army or anything ordinary. His work is secret. Grampa works for him and manages the warehouse, which travels along the line and moves every few miles.

We keep a home place in Louisiana, outside of New Orleans near Mandeville, but we only live there when I go school, or when we can't follow where Daddy is working. Gramma and Grampa live in the next little town down the road a couple of miles. Gramma says we shouldn't travel so much, because we have too many little kids, and that makes it hard for Mama. Mama says it's not like we aren't always going to have a baby, so that shouldn't keep us from traveling with Daddy.

And anyway, we take a house with us. A house-trailer, big and shiny, that we pull right behind the car, or that Daddy has somebody pull behind a truck if he can't be with us on the road. In the summertime, we don't go on vacation, we go live somewhere new. It's easy if you have a trailer house. When it is time to move, we just duct-tape all the cabinets and closets and drawers shut so our stuff doesn't fall out, and we hit the road. Mama has a whole extra house full of stuff like sheets, towels, dishes, and pots and pans that just stay in the trailer all the time. At the house, we drape old sheets on everything to keep the dust off when we're gone, and in the trailer, we just take the tape off everything when we are ready to move in. Gramma and Grampa have a little trailer that Grampa can pull right behind the Desoto.

When we get to where we're going, there's usually a trailer park where people already live, or the company sets up a lot with everything we need, like electricity and water. Sometimes the towns are littler or bigger than ours, but none of them are close to a big city as special as New Orleans.

You can almost tell if a town will be friendly or not by where we set up the trailers. If it is way out of town, close to the pipeline, we know the people in town want nothing to do with us except for what Gramma calls *floozies*, which I think must mean real friendly ladies. They come out and visit the men living on their own who must be awful sad missing their families. Sometimes, there's other families with kids we can play with, but mostly not. Mama says it's better if we don't play with the other company families, since Daddy is the boss and the welders or somebody are always on strike.

If the people in town are friendly and the town is big enough, sometimes we don't even need the trailers, because they rent houses and rooms to us. But lots of little towns aren't so friendly. They don't want us to play with their kids or go to their stores or live anywhere near them. They don't trust people who move around a lot, and think everyone should live in the same town where they were born their whole life. I've never even visited the town where I was born. Daddy and Granny can't even remember the name of the town where he was born. Mama says being well-traveled makes you a more interesting person, so I guess that's us. Other people call us ugly names, like gypsies and trailer trash. Mama says they are just ignorant, and that we should try to understand that people who haven't been anywhere don't know any better. Mama says it is just best if we keep to ourselves. Then there won't be any problems.

The trailer has all kinds of hiding places in it. Mamma and Daddy have a bedroom with an accordion door just like the instrument, but it doesn't make music. It fastens with a strap, and snaps right to the wall. I want a door like that on my bedroom at home, but Mama says no. Our beds are in the hallway and lift up so our clothes can be stored underneath them. The baby sleeps in the port-a-crib, which usually stays in the back seat of the car but comes inside the trailer when we're not driving. It sits right in the kitchen, once you fold the dinner table up against the wall.

The best part of the trailer is that the sofa opens out into a bed. Sometimes, if we are really good, Mama lets us sleep in the sofa bed. It has a storage space up underneath it that you can get to from inside or outside. Whenever people come to visit, especially town people, I feel like we have secrets they'll never understand, because they live in plain houses with ordinary furniture and closets. For now, while they still fit, Henry David and Samuel Taylor sleep end-to-end in the bed in the hall across from me. Everything is so snug, just like a dollhouse. Mama says it is perfect, because there is even room for a rocking chair. She says the only problem is that if she is going to sweep she has to pile us up on the furniture so she doesn't sweep all her children away with the mud that Daddy tracks in.

Sometimes, the towns we live in are so small or so unfriendly that we make our own entertainment. If Daddy is working late, Mama and some of the other wives load up the kids and we go to the drive-in movies, if there's one close enough. If it is a double screen, where you can see the movie at both ends of the parking lot, we put the back seats down in somebody's station wagon and all the kids lay in the way back and watch the movie. You just fall asleep there and wake up in your own bed like magic.

The single men and the married men whose families aren't with them all live together, away from the rest of us. Sometimes they drink beer and make too much noise—that's why we live apart from them. Both Mama and Gramma made us promise never to go near their trailers, and not to talk to the floozies. I think that's a shame, because most of the floozies are real friendly and real pretty, too. Some of them sit out in lawn chairs in the shade near the men's trailers, talking and laughing and smoking cigarettes and drinking beer right out of the bottle. They watch the wives hauling groceries and hanging laundry, but they don't ever speak to them. Some of the floozies have been with us for a couple of warehouse moves. They don't go to church and sometimes are sitting and smoking, still not dressed, just wearing silky wrappers, fuzzy mules dangling off their painted toes, when we get back from Sunday dinner.

If there are enough of us and we are going to be there for a while, Daddy has Grampa and some of the men lay down a good-sized concrete slab, put up an open shed, and run water and electricity to it. Then they stick a couple of washing machines in there so the wives don't have to take the laundry into town. Grampa also strings up clotheslines so they can hang laundry, rain or shine. The ladies and the floozies all like that, and fuss over him and bring him food Gramma won't let him eat because of his bad heart.

Grampa comes over after dinner almost every Saturday night whether we are home or on the road, because Gramma only wants to watch *Dragnet* and *Perry Mason* and Grampa likes to watch variety shows where you get to see singers and dancers and plate-spinners and sometimes a ventriloquist or dogs that wear clothes and dance. Grampa's favorite show is beauty pageants. He almost always picks the winner every time. Grampa does admire a pretty girl.

CHAPTER FIVE

⤙ ⤙

1959 — Train Station

I LIKE TO GO DOWNTOWN to the train station no matter who we're picking up. It's always cool in there, and a little darker than the outside. At the top of the stairs, my daddy asks how many, and since I forgot I was supposed to count, I say eleven, my favorite number, and he just says, "uh huh," which means he didn't count, either, so I'm not in trouble for not paying attention again, because none of my grownups are paying much attention these days.

I don't understand why they put all these steps up on the outside and more steps going down to the platforms on the inside, when they could've just built it all on one level and saved everybody a whole lot of trouble, but I don't tell my daddy because I'm not supposed to worry about stuff like that.

"Evening, Roscoe."

"Evening, Mr. Pete. Evening, Miss DG. Y'all got company coming?"

I like Roscoe, and I wish my daddy wore a uniform to work like he does, instead of just a shirt and tie. I like the way Roscoe says "DiGi," stretching it out like a real name and not just like initials, DG, which it is. Roscoe touches the brim of his cap and bends just a little at the waist.

I say, "Evening, Roscoe" back to him, and nod my head like grownup ladies do and try to remember all the stuff I'm not supposed to do, like call him Mister or curtsy or ask how he keeps his teeth so white.

"Train from Chicago on time, Roscoe?" my daddy asks.

Roscoe says, "Yes, sir, Mr. Pete. Due in at 8:59. Your mama coming for a visit?"

My daddy nods yes and helps me scoot up on the bench. I'm busy arranging skirts and petticoats so nothing wrinkles and trying to figure out a way to tell if you really can see my underwear in my patent leather shoes, which Gramma's always warning me about. My daddy sits down beside me, stretches out his long legs, and pushes his hat back on his head just a little.

"Roscoe, you got a girl can help my mama?"

When we live up north, my daddy hires a maid, but here at home, somebody comes in to help. The only difference I can tell is what we call the women who come to work. We didn't have any help before my mama had to go away, and I think my daddy feels bad about that on account of her being so tired, and he wants to be sure she doesn't get that way again.

Roscoe's thinking real hard about what my daddy asked him, and he's trying to figure out if he knows anybody he can get to work for Granny, because she about ran through all his relatives last time she was here. My daddy even had to promise Franklin, Roscoe's boy who plays baseball for the colored school, that he can come do the yard work on Sunday mornings when Granny's in church, so he won't have to see her all summer.

"I'll send somebody over in the morning, Mr. Pete. I can find somebody your mama can't run off." Roscoe grins real big, and he and my daddy laugh, but I'm not so sure Roscoe knows anybody my Granny can't run off.

Roscoe checks his pocket watch and squints, comparing it with the big clock on the wall, and says, "Train's coming, Mr. Pete. We best get ready." My daddy puts his hands on his knees and pushes himself up kind of slow. He turns and picks me up under the arms and swings me onto Roscoe's cart.

"Hold on tight, Miss DiGi," says Roscoe, and I grab the bar between his big hands, and he pushes off and we sail down the platform toward the light.

This is my favorite part, the train coming in. I see the light moving closer, the noise gets louder and louder, and the screeching starts, and I wonder if the brakeman ever just forgets and lets the train keep running right on through to New Orleans and on without stopping, right on into the ocean.

Roscoe and my daddy are leaning in toward each other and laughing at something I can't hear, because now I have my hands over my ears. The train's so loud, and steam is billowing everywhere like a dragon in one of the stories my mama reads me, huge and fierce and loud and scary, and just for a minute, I miss my mama awful, so awful my stomach hurts, but the train just goes slower and slower and the noise gets louder and louder and the steam thicker and thicker.

My daddy leans over, hollers, "You ready?" and lifts me down off the cart. It's my job to get Granny.

"Come on, Roscoe!" I grab his hand and we start trying to figure out which car she's in, because the trick is to find her first. The train's already stopping, there's another burst of steam, and there's my Granny in the doorway one car down, already waving her hanky with one hand and holding her flat black hat on with the other, her big old Marshall Field's shopping bag clanking on her arm. She's dressed all in black, shiny straw hat to lace-up shoes, her hair a white cloud that just blends right in with all the steam.

Me and Roscoe are almost running now, but I can tell we're not gonna make it. Granny's got the steward trapped behind her so he can't get out and put the steps down. She opens her mouth and hollers louder than the train, louder than the steam, louder than everything,

"Alcide! Alcide Louis! Alcide Louis! Are you out there?" Granny always gets off the train like we're gonna miss her in the crowd, even when she's the only one getting off.

Roscoe and me make it in time to keep her from hollering again. I'm grinning because I know my daddy's back there somewhere, pretending to be invisible. He hates his name, and nobody, not nobody but Granny ever uses it. Except for every once in a while, my mama does, and Daddy chases her and Mama lets him catch her and they hug and laugh and laugh. My stomach hurts again, but I've got Granny to deal with right now, and Granny takes a lot of dealing with.

The steward finally just gives up on getting Granny out of his way and hands the steps over her head to Roscoe, which he can do because she's so tiny.

Roscoe helps her down to the platform, saying, "Evening, Miz Pitre. Welcome back."

Roscoe's about the politest person I know, and Granny appreciates polite. She nods at Roscoe, turns to me, hands over her shopping bag, spits on her hanky, wipes at some imaginary dirt on my face because I surely know better than to have a dirty face around Granny, brushes her dry lips across the spot and says, "Where's your daddy, girl?" She smells like Vicks and Listerine and bleach and talcum powder and Granny.

I love to watch her with my daddy, because she treats him like he's about my age and not at all like somebody's grown up, movie-star-handsome Daddy. I laugh. "Hey, Granny. How was your trip?" I ask her.

Granny's never had a good trip as far as I can tell, and she's watching like a hawk while Roscoe loads hatboxes and suitcases and even a trunk onto his cart. Granny doesn't think anybody does a good job at anything unless she's watching, so she watches everybody all the time.

I've got her shopping bag pulled with both hands up under my chin so it won't drag on the ground, and it's bouncing off my knees and clanging and rattling something awful. Granny carries all her cleaning supplies in case she has to use the public restroom somewhere, and you have to be real careful not to drop the bag or tear it, or all kinds of embarrassing stuff rolls out everywhere.

Now that she's done hollering his name in front of everybody, my daddy shows up. "Hello, Mama!" He bends almost in half so she can hug his neck.

Granny finally lets him go, but reaches up to touch his cheek, tilts her head, looks at him real hard, and says, "All right, Alcide Louis Pitre. What kind of a mess you got yourself now?"

CHAPTER SIX

⊷ ⊷

1959 — Granny and Flozella

GRANNY AND FLOZELLA stand on the sleeping porch, just inside the screen doors, in the noisy comfort of the ceiling fans that squeak and wobble overhead. I sit on the stoop outside but I can hear them clearly, and I am taking notes for my daddy, who wants to know all about this meeting, which he says is like President Eisenhower meeting with Khrushchev, a meeting of Cold War giants, whatever that means.

Flozella is certainly a giant. She towers over everybody, including my daddy, who is usually the tallest person in the room. She has legs like tree trunks and feet that never seem to fit her shoes, which she takes off as soon as she is inside the house. This drives Granny crazy. She thinks bare feet are nasty, and while she wants you to take your outdoor shoes off at the door, she wants you to put on house shoes right away, even if you're wearing socks.

Next to Flozella, Granny looks like an antique doll wearing a black dress, black stockings, black lace-up shoes, and an apron that practically covers everything she's got on. She pulls her white hair into a knot on top her head and fastens it with just one pin, then puts a white hairnet over the whole thing. We buy those hairnets in paper packages of three at the Five and Dime, and put them in her stocking at Christmas time. My mama stocks up on them whenever they have them in white to match Granny's hair. She keeps a drawer full of things to give as presents, like Gramma's favorite perfume, Tabu, and Grampa's sock garters, which he's always breaking or using for something other than holding up his socks. There's little toys for the boys—cowboys and Indians or soldiers. For me, she has paper dolls or special drawing paper and pencils, not just school paper and writing pencils. For Daddy, she keeps monogrammed handkerchiefs and lighter fluid and an extra Zippo with his initials on it. Whenever she gives a present, she replaces it with something new.

But my mama's not here now, and I've got to quit daydreaming and pay attention to what's going on in front of me.

Granny barely comes up to Flozella's elbow. Flozella even makes me feel tiny, even though I'm already taller than Granny, coming up on being as tall as my mama and Gramma. Flozella is broad, too. She fills up most of the doorways in the house and has to crouch down to get into the attic. When she rides the bus to our house, she takes up most of a whole row of seats.

Roscoe has sent Flozella to help Granny while my mama is away. It took him almost a week to find somebody who would come. Granny has a reputation for being hard to get along with. She's real particular about how things get done around the house. It is a lot of work to keep house with so many kids running around, especially boys.

Granny and Flozella are standing on the steps that lead from the sleeping porch to the back yard. Granny near the top, Flozella down in the yard, so they are at eye-level. I sit on the steps between them so I can watch both of them.

"No clothesline?" Flozella asks. Granny shakes her head, and Flozella, silent for now, echoes her movement. I interrupt to tell them that we have a brand-new gas clothes dryer in the house, and don't need a clothesline anymore.

Granny just wags her finger at me and my notepad, and says, "Write clothesline down on your list. Clothes smell nasty if they are dried in a machine." I confine my grumbling to my head. Maybe my daddy can explain better about the clothes dryer than I can.

"Room for a garden, too. Down along the fence at the bottom of the yard," Flozella weighs in, and now I'm going to have explain about frozen vegetables. We have a whole freezer of them.

"Where's Roscoe's boy? Doesn't he come around anymore?" asks Granny. Flozella's looking at me with a little smile sneaking around her mouth. I know better than to tell Granny, that Franklin's so scared of her that he won't come around, if there's even a chance he'll run into her.

"He comes around, Miz Pitre. I have Roscoe get on to him tonight. He show up tomorrow, and plant us some poles for a clothesline. Mr. LeBreton, over to the hardware store, got some." Flozella's voice is deep and musical. She sings in the Antioch African Methodist Episcopal Church choir, louder than everybody else put together. "It's late to plant anything,"

Flozella observes, not really challenging Granny. Just letting her know what she thinks.

"Seeds. Put down seeds," Granny directs. "Tomato, beans...." Granny trails off.

"Squash, collards, carrots, field peas...." Flozella adds. I scribble all this down, not sure about the spelling, but can't stop myself from busting out, "We don't even eat those things!"

Daddy calls that stuff "poor food," and says he had plenty of it growing up and doesn't want it now that he can afford better. We eat things like LaSeur peas from a can and Green Giant corn from the freezer, and not from a cob.

Granny huffs, "You'll eat what you're served." Flozella just stares down at me like I ought to know better.

"Chickens," she says. "No use to pay for eggs. Franklin can build us a coop." This time, it's Granny nodding in agreement.

So far, this is not working out like I expected. I thought Granny'd have a whole list of unreasonable requirements, and Flozella would throw up her hands and walk out, like Orletta did the last time Granny came to stay. Of course, we haven't done the inside, yet.

We move indoors, and I sit at the wooden table while Granny talks about indoor chores. "Laundry every day, towels, diapers, children's clothes. Sheets for the whole house, twice a week. Ironed before they go back on the beds. Rest of the ironing can be done once a week on Thursdays. Except for Mr. Pitre's work clothes. Starched and ironed every day, including his undershirts and shorts, not starched, just ironed. Fold his socks, don't ball them. That's the way he likes it." Granny continues the list as I scribble furiously to keep up. "I do my own laundry. You don't need to touch my things. When my daughter-in-law gets home, we won't need you every day. Just three days a week. You and she will work that out."

I can see Flozella bristle a little at this. She doesn't know that Granny doesn't like anybody touching her things. Maybe I can tell her later. She probably doesn't understand about my mama, either.

Granny starts to tell Flozella how she wants the rest of the house kept, but is interrupted. "Miz Pitre, I been keep ing house for folks near as long as you. I know when to do what and how to do it. Sweep and mop every day. Dust every other. Keep an eye on the children and make sure they get fed. Keep an eye on they mama when she get home. Cook when you don't want to. I know it all. If the ironing gets to be too much, I take it home get my sister to help. We'll work it out. I be here after breakfast on the weekdays and stay till after supper. Except Wednesdays. I got choir practice and church. I need a half-day on Wednesdays. I'll come special for extra on Saturdays, but you got to let me know. I don't work on Sundays. Ever." Flozella's voice is firm but respectful. She knows her way around white folks. Granny and Flozella don't talk about money. My daddy has already handled that.

Chapter Seven

꘠ ꘠

1959 — *Brownies*

THIS IS THE MOST EXCITING DAY OF MY LIFE! The
Brownies are meeting at my house. It's not like this happens every day. With as many girls as there are in my troop,
we meet someplace different every time, and not always at
somebody's house. Sometimes we meet in the community
center, which smells like feet, and sometimes we meet in the
school cafeteria, which is the worst, since it always smells like
boiled wienies. But today we are meeting at my house.

Me and Mama have been working all week on getting
ready. We get to wear our uniforms to school, so mine had
to be washed and ironed just right and has been hanging on
my bedroom door since Sunday night. I keep my hat stuffed
with tissue so it doesn't get crushed, and Mama has given me

a hatbox to keep it in and I brush it just so, so there isn't a speck of dust on it. Then the house needs to be perfect, and let me tell you, with two boys and the baby, that isn't easy. Every time I get something straightened up, they mess it up again. I don't wonder that Mama is tired all the time.

I want everything just perfect. I get that from Mama. My bedroom is everything I ever dreamed of. It has a pink carpet and ballet dancers on the bedspread and curtains. The dancers are from a painting in a book that Mama showed me when we were picking stuff out for redecorating. The painting is by Edgar Degas, and it is called *Dancers in Pink*. It's the most beautiful thing I've ever seen. The dancers are dressed in pink and blue, and the stage lights shine all over them. I want to be a ballerina when I grow up, but Madame Louise says she can already tell I'll be too tall and sticks me in the back row. It's my feet. You can always tell by the feet, she says. Also, my tutu droops no matter how much we starch it. I think it has already given up.

We have snacks and Kool-Aid all ready before I even leave for school. Henry David and Samuel Taylor and the baby, Oscar Fingal, will be sent to the next-door neighbor's house after school so they can't interrupt anything. I hurry home as soon as school lets out so I can be a proper hostess and greet everybody as they arrive. The minute I hit our street, I see two cars parked in front of our house. That's the troop leader and a helper mother who'll keep things running smoothly for my mother, who is responsible for this meeting.

We always start with some business stuff, like the pledge and the law. "I will try to do my best, to do my duty to God and my country…" and "A Brownie is honest. A Brownie is trustworthy…." If there's a flag around, we say that pledge, too. Then we read something from *The Girl Scout Handbook*.

We catch up on who's working on what badges, and some-times we work as a group, so everybody gets the same badge—like first aid, when we took turns bandaging each other and setting imaginary broken legs. Last year, we all got a camping badge, and never even had to leave our backyard to do it. Grampa pretended to be a bear in the middle of the night so we could practice our survival skills.

Last month, we made sit-upons, foam cushions that we use on the floor or the ground to be more comfortable. Somebody's mother brought the foam, and mine brought the covers. She took yards and yards of canvas fabric, and for each girl in the troop, drew a picture of them and let-tered their Indian name underneath it. My Indian name is *E-ha-weeh*, which means Laughing Maiden, and that's the picture Mama drew of me: laughing with my hair in braids and a headband. We had to figure out how to divide the foam into the right number of cushions, and then how to cut it, and then how to cut the canvas to cover the foam. Once we had everything measured and cut, we each had to paint the canvas faces before we glued them on the cush-ions. We were at the community center every week, where we worked on them, because nobody's mother wanted that much mess in their houses. We'll have the best sit-upons at the citywide jamboree at the end of the school year. We also got a badge for the project, but I can't remember which one. My sit-upon is already waiting for me in the living room at home.

As I get closer to the house, I see the helper mothers are standing at the front door with plates of cookies in their hands. Why hasn't Mama let them in? She was fine when I left for school this morning, really fine. She got everybody up, and she was listening to things we said and paying attention the whole time. The last thing she said to me before I left was, "Hope you like the surprise!"

"Hey, Mrs. Hebert, Mrs. Dolan. How come y'all are out here? Didn't Mama answer the door? She's probably out back, and didn't hear you knock." I don't like this, but I'm supposed to act like everything is perfect, no matter what. "Y'all come on in, and I'll find Mama."

I open the door and find the house decorated for this afternoon's meeting. There's a big sign that reads "Welcome Troop 106!" Nametags are set up on the dining room table, along with pastel-colored paper plates and matching cups, and little paper swans holding nuts and mints. Grampa and Mama spent a week folding them and then painting on their faces. In a few minutes, little girls like me will grab them and crumple them up when they are empty.

"I'll just check on Mama and be right back. Please make yourselves at home. She's probably just taken the boys next door so Mrs. Wiley can watch them."

I slip out the back door and across the yard to the neighbor's house. I knock once on their back door and step inside. Henry David and Samuel Taylor are sitting at the kitchen table eating baloney sandwiches. The baby, Oscar Fingal, sleeps on Flozella's hip while she rocks back and forth, stirring something on the stove. The boys are okay. That's good.

"Flozella, have you seen my mama?"

"She drop these boys off about an hour ago. She seem fine then."

"She should be ready for my Brownie meeting. And she's not."

"You didn't look for her in the house, did you, DG?"

"No, I came right away to check on the boys. But Mrs. Hebert and Mrs. Dolan are in the house and all the other girls and mothers are going to start showing up...." My voice is rising in panic. My chest is getting tight, and I wonder where my inhaler is. I know what to do if we are alone or if adults are coming, but not what to do when it's a bunch of my friends. We didn't plan for that. We didn't practice. It won't be perfect.

Flozella says, "Stop, child! You'll make yourself sick! We'll fix this. Find my shoes; they here somewhere." Flozella barrels out of the kitchen in search of Mrs. Wiley, who comes back with her, holding Finn.

"I do wish you'd keep your shoes on in the house, Flozella. Oh, hello, DG. I understand your Mama needs to borrow Flozella for a little bit. I had planned on her watching the boys and I need her back to finish dinner...." She's hesitant and flustered, and I need to get both Flozella and me out of here.

"She'll be right back, Mrs. Wiley. Not more than half an hour, I promise. Mama says thank you very much." A little white lie that doesn't hurt anything.

Flozella is respectful and nods in agreement. "I'll be back in plenty of time. These boys won't be any trouble while I'm gone." She sharply eyes Henry David and Samuel Taylor, who beam at Mrs. Wiley like little angels. She takes hold of my hand, squeezes it, and moves away.

Flozella, for all her size, is pretty fast as we scoot across the backyards to my house. As we reach the back door, she squeezes my hand tight again and hauls me up the back steps into our kitchen, where Mrs. Hebert and Mrs. Dolan are standing, looking concerned and guilty, as if they've been surprised in the middle of talking about something they shouldn't.

"Afternoon, ladies. Y'all find everything you need?" Flozella asks them. The doorbell rings. She looks down at me. "You know what to do, DG. Go greet your company. I'm going upstairs and check on your mama. I'll take care of everything. Ladies, why don't y'all settle the girls out on the sleeping porch. That'll be a good place for your meeting." She gives orders like a queen or a general, and nobody does anything but what she says to.

At the front door, girls are being dropped off, lugging sit-upons and sweaters and handbooks and cookies and other Brownie paraphernalia. We squeal and hug, and I tell them where to go, and Mary Frances, who is always early, helps direct the ones who don't know where the back porch is, and I keep looking up the stairs and listening to doors opening and closing and to the heavy tread of Flozella's very large feet. She would never make a ballerina, either.

The door opens, and this time, it's Grampa and Gramma, with her portable organ in tow. They drag it out to the sleeping porch, and Gramma sets it up. I guess Flozella must have called them from the telephone upstairs. Grampa comes back through the house, stops for a minute, and touches my face. "I love you, DG." Then he heads upstairs.

The doorbell rings again, and it is two stragglers, the Leary twins, whose mother never gets them anywhere on time. Dr. Levin and Father Mike follow them in. The doctor heads upstairs, and Father Mike stops long enough to say, "She's okay, DG. Everything will be fine. Join your friends."

I do as am I told. Everything has to be perfect.

Gramma plays the organ and sings parlor songs like "I'm Only a Bird in a Gilded Cage," and doesn't play one hymn.

When Grampa comes down, she goes up, and he makes a May basket with folded tissue paper and promises that as soon as the mothers decide they're up to it, he'll come back and teach us all how to make one. I hear the back door close, and watch Flozella cross the yard on her way back to Mrs. Wiley's. She carries a carefully bundled armload of darkly-stained sheets and towels.

The meeting comes to an end as we form a circle and cross our arms and sing "Make New Friends." Mothers and fathers start honking out front, and girls gather their things and head home. Some cradle paper-swan nut cups in their hands as if they were made of gold.

Grampa takes a plate of cookies to Mrs. Wiley when he goes to get the boys. Flozella does not come back with him. She has dinner to serve.

Gramma cooks hamburger patties and canned peas, and we talk about everything except Mama. We all pretend that the meeting was perfect, and that half the town doesn't wonder what is going on at our house.

Gramma is getting the boys ready for bed and Grampa is helping me with my arithmetic homework when Doctor Levin comes down. The adults talk in the hall for a few minutes, and Grampa wants to know when my daddy will be home. But he hasn't been for a couple of nights, and the work may keep him away again tonight, and I don't know. I just don't know. I should know.

The doctor leaves, and later, when I am supposed to be asleep in my room, another man arrives, someone I don't know. He goes upstairs to my mama's room at the end of the hall and comes back down the stairs with a small bundle in his arms. I stand behind my bedroom door and watch him through the crack. Father Mike follows him to the front door.

When he comes back upstairs, Father Mike stops at my door and asks through the crack, "Aren't you supposed to be asleep?"

"Yes, sir."

"Do you plan on standing behind the door all night?"

"No, sir."

"Your mother will be fine. She's just a little under the weather. She'll be herself in a couple of days. Oh, and we found your father. He's on his way home. Your mother is sleeping now. So should you be."

"Okay."

"Don't forget to say your prayers."

"Yes, sir."

"Goodnight."

I kneel beside the bedspread with its perfect dancers in my perfect room, and say my perfect prayers: "God bless Mama and Daddy and Gramma and Grampa and Granny and Henry David and Samuel Taylor and Oscar Fingal and the baby who will never have a name."

CHAPTER EIGHT

❧ ❧

1960 — *Being Polite*

THE CAR IS MORE CROWDED THAN USUAL, with Daddy, Granny, and Mama in the front seat and me between Gramma and Grampa in the back. Granny's second-best hat just peeks over the edge of the seat in front of me, and I wonder how much trouble I can be in if it only merits her second-best hat. Gramma just has an everyday hat on. Mama wears a lace scarf, and Daddy and Grampa wear their usual Stetsons. Grampa's is square and stocky, like him, while Daddy's is lean and long. My favorite part of their hats is the little card that fits in the hatband on the inside. One side says *Stetson Hat Company* with a name and address and a special hat number, and the other says "Like hell it's yours! Put it back," with their names printed up in big red letters.

Ladies' hats don't have anything nearly so interesting on the inside, just the name of the hat maker, like Lily Daché. No way to tell who the hat belongs to, and no swearing. I don't have a hat on at all, not even a chapel scarf.

It's awful quiet in the car, with no radio and nobody talking much. Now and then, Granny lets out a big sigh and dabs at her face with her handkerchief. I can't see that, except in my head, but I know what she looks like when she's aggravated at me. I try one more time to explain. "I was just trying to be polite."

Grampa squeezes my knee, makes a snorting sound, and looks out the window. Daddy coughs and sputters a little, and squirms some in the driver's seat. Gramma *harrumphs* and Granny sighs some more, and her handkerchief flutters. Mama looks over her shoulder, shakes her head slightly, and looks back out her window. I don't think everybody needs to be wearing hats. It's only the middle of the week, and hats just make everything seem more important.

Sometimes it seems like I can't do anything right, no matter how hard I try. And now we all have to go meet with Father Mike to see if he can fix this, and it really wasn't my fault. I was just trying to be polite.

Patty Miller's birthday always comes just after school is out for the summer and it is still easy to get everyone together for a party. Every year, her mother lets her choose one girl to spend the night with her after the party. Everyone always wants to be that girl, and this year, it was me.

I'd never been so excited about a party before. Mama and I bought the perfect present, which I knew, because Patty told me exactly what to buy. I had a new shorts-set to wear, with a matching bucket hat so I wouldn't sunburn, and I got to pick the color, and even if it was wrong for me, Mama let me get it anyway. I had my own round Annette Funicello overnight bag and pink shorty pajamas and a travel toothbrush with a little tiny tube of toothpaste. I packed and unpacked every night for a week to be sure I had everything, and even made a list of things that would have to go in at the last minute, like my hairbrush and my pillow and extra underpants, because you can never have too many underpants. I had so many things to keep track of that I was sure I'd forget something important, like the birthday present, or the card that said it was from me, or something that would ruin the whole thing. Mama kept telling me not to worry, that she wouldn't let me forget anything.

At the party, we ate cake and played games and ran through the sprinkler until it was time for all the other girls to go home. Patty and I went to her bedroom and played with all her new stuff until Mrs. Miller called us to dinner. I'm always nervous about dinner at other people's houses, because I'm kind of a picky eater and I don't like my food to touch. Mama says I must eat everything people put in front of me, not ask for seconds, and always tell the hostess how good it was. When I asked if that wasn't the same as lying, she just looked at me and told me to do as she said, no ifs, ands, or buts.

Luckily, we had cold ham, potato salad, the good kind with hard-boiled eggs and pickle relish, and sweet tea. We all— Patty, her mama and daddy, and her older brother, who is in high school, and me—ate out on the patio in the backyard, with paper plates just like a picnic. Granny says only heathens eat dinner outside, but I don't think the Millers are heathens, exactly, even if they are Protestants. Granny wasn't sure if I should spend the night, but Mrs. Miller promised to bring me home before they went to church on Sunday morning.

The Millers go to the Baptist church where Gramma plays the piano and the organ on Sunday. I said I could just come home with Gramma, but Granny wouldn't hear of it.

Once we finished dinner and threw away our dishes, Mrs. Miller said to wash up and get in the car. As we headed to Patty's room, I heard Mr. Miller ask Mrs. Miller if she thought this was a good idea. I didn't hear her answer, but soon we were loaded up in the car and headed out for a drive into the country. Patty and I talked the whole time, until we were stopping with a bunch of other cars all parked around a great big tent. It looked like people must have come from all around to see the circus.

As we got out of the car, I got pretty excited. I sure would have something to tell the other girls when I saw them next week at the swimming pool. None of them got to go to the circus with Patty Miller. Then I remembered that the swimming pool was closed this summer on account of polio, and I didn't know when I would see them again. But this was such juicy news that it would last just fine until school started again. I just hoped we'd still live here in September.

As we walked toward the tent, I began to wonder what kind of circus or carnival this might be. I couldn't smell popcorn or animals, and the music didn't sound like a circus. People, especially the ladies, seemed excited, but the kids and most of the husbands kind of trudged along. At the flap to the tent, some men were handing out little books, so I took one and followed the Millers in. Patty and me sat with her parents while her brother found a seat in the back with some of his friends. When I got settled next to Patty, I checked out my little souvenir book, and was surprised to find out it was a Bible of some kind with a bunch of the words written in red. It had the thinnest paper pages I had ever seen in a book, which made it real hard to read, since you could see two pages at once.

Things got real interesting fast. There was loud music and singing and clapping, and lots of *hallelujahs* and *Amens*. The man up front, Patty told me he was called a preacher, yelled at us about sinning and all the terrible things that would happen to us if we didn't change our heathen ways. I remembered we had eaten dinner outside and got a little worried, but since I had only done it once, I didn't think I was in too much trouble.

The shouting seemed to go on forever and people began to mill around, some standing up and raising up their hands, some talking funny (Patty said it was called *tongues*), some wandering out into the aisle, falling down, and jerking around. It was the most entertaining church service I'd ever been to. It was nothing like Father Mike's masses, where he speaks mostly in Latin. I wondered, *is that the same as tongues?* Nobody ever rolled in the aisle during mass, and I'm pretty sure Sister Margaret would whack you with a ruler if you just hollered out *Amen* or *hallelujah*. This was like being at the movies, where you never knew what was going to happen next.

I quit trying to keep up with what the preacher was saying, and just watched the goings-on. Sometimes I had to ask a question about what was happening, but I tried not to seem too surprised, and to be polite. Mrs. Miller sat swaying beside me, and I could see the sweat running down her neck. She occasionally let loose with a ladylike "Amen," or raised one hand in the air and shook it, but I didn't expect her to roll in the aisle anytime soon. I was beginning to be a little bored, and had closed my eyes for just a minute when I felt a hand on my shoulder.

"Are you feeling it?" Mrs. Miller asked. "Are you feeling the Holy Spirit?"

Mostly what I felt was hot and sweaty and tired. It had been a real long day. Remembering my marching orders to eat everything, even if the food was touching, and to always be polite, I answered, "Yes, ma'am."

Well, boy, did Mrs. Miller get excited! She jumped up, waved her hands in the air, and called out for an usher. Patty was gushing all over me about how it hadn't happened to her yet, and she was so jealous and she couldn't hardly wait. I began to wonder just what I'd gotten myself into when a man showed up and Mrs. Miller handed me off to him, saying, "You'll be just fine. He'll bring you right back here."

I got marched up to the front of the tent, where it turned out there was a great big tub of water. You know how you know when you've messed up, but you don't know how, exactly? That feeling was crawling all over me. I couldn't see a way out of this, whatever it was, without drawing attention. Some ladies took me behind a screen and shucked me out of my clothes and into some kind of sheet. I'm not used to being undressed by strangers, but I remembered to be polite. There was a lot of *Praise Jesus*-ing and *Thank the Lord*s, and somebody I couldn't see remarked as to how this would show the Catholics just whose side God was really on.

Once they had me wrapped in the sheet, they hustled me back out front. I got moved to the front of the line like they thought I might cut and run, which was becoming likelier by the minute. It felt like everybody was looking at me, and I began to think maybe this wasn't something I ought to get involved in. Some adult kept their hand on me the whole time, so I couldn't figure out how to get away. I recognized most of the people I could see from around town: Mr. Hebert from the grocery store, Mr. Williams from the filling station, a couple of mothers I knew from Brownies. They all looked a little different in the way that people do when you see them somewhere else.

There was already a big red-faced man in a white robe standing in the tub, along with a couple of other men I didn't know. Mr. Williams picked me up, said, "Don't you be afraid!" and handed me over to the strangers. They lifted me up and stood me in the tub, and then somebody was praying over me. They tipped me over backwards and dunked me under real quick. Then, just as fast, I was out of the tub, dragged behind the screen again, dried off with a towel I was pretty sure Granny wouldn't approve of, stuffed back into my clothes, and marched back to Patty and her family. Somebody stuck a certificate in my hand stating that I was now and forever a Baptist. Uh oh. I was pretty sure that Catholics are not supposed to be Baptists.

The singing and praying and stuff went on for a lot longer. As we trooped back across the dusty parking lot, people kept coming up to Mrs. Miller and congratulating her on saving me, and telling her how much it meant to everyone to see me rescued from Satan. It made me feel funny, but I still tried to be polite. Mrs. Miller preened and blessed and told them the Lord chose her to aid in his work, she was just a tool. Only Mr. Miller asked what she planned to tell my grandmothers, and told her not to expect him to clean up any of her mess.

The next morning, we got up early so the Millers could get me home before they had to be at church. I was already saying my thank-yous and ready to run up the front walk when Mr. Miller told his wife that she needed to walk me to the door and explain. I got the feeling he thought she was in trouble. I could already see Granny just inside the screen door, watching suspiciously as we trailed up the walk. Granny was pretty much always suspicious of everybody, and I think Mrs. Miller set her back teeth grating.

I scampered up the walk fast as I could, hoping to get in and out of the way, and kissed Granny quick, but she hooked the screen door shut and got ahold of my shoulder tight at the same time.

Mrs. Miller beamed a "Good Morning, sister," at my Granny, who coldly nodded back and didn't unhook the screen door. This was already off to a bad start.

Granny looked down at me, squeezed my shoulder even tighter, and asked, "Did you thank Mr. and Mrs. Miller?"

"Yes, ma'am."

She peered out at Mrs. Miller challengingly and waited. Mrs. Miller ploughed on. "Why, you can't imagine the Good News!" She said it with Capital Letters. Granny just stood there, one hand on her cheek and the other about to pulverize my collarbone.

"Last night, after the party, we took the girls with us over to the revival in Lake Providence. It was just packed with people and filled with the Spirit of the Lord. Everyone felt it. I was so surprised and pleased when DG said she felt it, too! Why, she just marched up there like a soldier of the Lord and accepted Jesus Christ as her Lord and Savior. It was just wonderful!"

Mrs. Miller was running out of steam in the face of Granny's rock-hard silence, but she kept smiling and waiting for Granny to praise the Lord or hallelujah in return. Instead, she got "Thank you for having her to your house and for bringing her home." And then she got our backs as Granny steered me down the shotgun hall and out of sight.

By now, I was up on my tiptoes, with my shoulders inched up around my ears. Granny whipped me around to face her, and grabbed both arms like she was fixing to shake me. "What have you done?" she hissed.

Since I wasn't quite sure, I handed her my certificate and answered, "I was just being polite."

This occasioned an outburst such as I had never seen. My tiny granny was shaking furiously and spitting the most vehement Hail Mary I'd ever heard, broken only by the calling of my daddy's name: "Alcide! Alcide Louis! Git in here now."

Mama's head appeared out of a doorway. She and my daddy arrived in the parlor at the same time, Mama with the baby on her hip and a book in one hand, Daddy wearing an apron and carrying a wooden spoon. Things just kept getting worse! Daddy was cooking gumbo, and I didn't know where my inhaler was. Usually, I go over to the neighbors when Daddy cooks, because of my allergies.

"What's got your hair on fire, Mama?" Daddy asked her while eyeing me suspiciously.

Granny brandished my certificate like she wanted to whip me with it. Usually, a certificate was a pretty good thing. I got them all the time. Not today. She handed it off to Daddy, who read it and passed it on to Mama, who rescued me from Granny's clutch and was rubbing my sore shoulder. Mama's hand was shaking, and Daddy had his hand over his mouth. Mama asked, "How did this happen, DG?"

I explained about the tent that wasn't a circus, and people rolling in the aisles and getting dunked, and ended with my best and truest reason: "You told me to be polite. I was just being polite!"

I got excused to go to my room and found my inhaler. I didn't close the door all the way, so I could still hear them, especially Granny, who was louder than Mama and Daddy combined. She seemed to be concerned about my immortal soul, while Mama was worried about what Gramma and Grampa would think. Daddy must have been laughing, because Granny told him he needed to take this seriously, and that he had better figure out what to do about it pretty quick.

That was how we all ended up in the car on the way to see Father Mike.

Father Mike knows Gramma and Grampa from before he was a priest, when they were all young together. Gramma even has a picture of him and Grampa from college. They both wear football jerseys and hold funny-looking leather helmets. They almost look like brothers, with their dark, slicked-back hair and wide smiles. Father Mike went on to seminary, and Grampa, well, he drank a lot, had some heart attacks, and became Grampa who fixes broken things. Father Mike kept his hair and Grampa's losing his, but if you squint just right, you can see the boys they used to be.

There's a lot of shaking and howdying once we get to the church. Father Mike takes us all into his study, and I explain again what happened and how I was just being polite. His face is very serious as he listens, and he ignores the noises that my grownups make—snorts from Grampa and Daddy, a small cough from my mama, *tsks* and outraged sighs from both grandmothers. He asks if I have my certificate with me. I hand it to him, a little crumpled and sweaty. He smooths it on the flat surface of his desk and reads it carefully. When he finishes, he tents his hands and bows his head slightly like he's praying.

When he raises his head, his face is still serious, but his eyes are twinkling at me. "So, DG, did you know what you were agreeing to when this was going on?"

"No, sir! I surely didn't! I just didn't want to make a fuss in front of all those people. I was just trying to be polite!" All this just bursts out of me like an explosion.

"Well, I think we can take care of this right now." Father Mike is still twinkling, and Daddy and Grampa are nudging each other like they are a couple of little boys misbehaving in church, which I guess they are. My mama isn't paying any attention to what's going on, and I'm afraid of what that means. Both grandmothers are keeping a keen eye on me and Father Mike, in case we try to get away with something.

Father Mike parades the lot of us out to the church and up to the stoup. He sprinkles holy water on my head, rests his hand it, and chants solemnly for a long time in Latin. None of us can understand him. Then he asks us all to join him in the Lord's Prayer. Finally, he assigns my grandmothers an unholy number of Hail Marys, and tells my mama to be especially watchful of me. I am strictly forbidden to get baptized again under any circumstances, even if I must be rude about it. That seems real unfair, but I think this might be a good time to keep my mouth shut.

We all troop back to Father Mike's office, where he uses a big stamp to mark my certificate "cancelled." He hands it to my mother and tells her to save it with my birth certificate and other important papers.

The trip home is a little more relaxed, what with both grandmothers *Hail Marying* their hearts out. I try to explain one last time that I was just being polite, while my daddy and Grampa still act like little boys, and my mama stares into the distance. I wonder what I can do to call her back.

CHAPTER NINE

⊷ ⊷

1960 — Cemetery Day

SATURDAY IS FULL OF DEAD. The garden is full of dead plants that need to be weeded and cleaned up so new stuff can be planted. There are unexplained dead birds lying in the front yard, and the dog looks completely innocent and that he'd like to be sure we remember that he slept in the boys' room last night. There's a dead skunk somewhere nearby, but not too close.

Even the car battery is dead, and I don't think Daddy noticed it was because somebody left the headlights on. Sometimes, I am allowed to read in the car in the evenings if the boys are being especially rowdy. I like to pretend that I am driving the big black car with fins like a Flash Gordon spaceship, and everybody knows you can't drive a car after dark without the lights on.

Granny and I are ready to go visiting. Daddy and Grampa get the car running again without too much trouble, and we don't even lose much time. Daddy pulls out of the driveway, irritated anyway. He's always irritated on Cemetery Day. It won't take him but a little while to make up the time we lost while he was getting the car started, and when he gets to drive fast, he forgets to be irritated.

I read a book in the backseat, which seems huge without the boys. Everything is bigger and quieter without the boys. I don't have to worry too much about getting wrinkled, because it doesn't matter how I look at the cemetery.

I can just barely see Granny's hat over the back of the front seat. The noise of the car's big engine mostly drowns out the sound of their voices. I think they might be arguing about something, which means Granny is ready to go back to her other home with Daddy's sister, Aunt Odilia. She never just says she's ready to go back; she gets all mad and picks a fight with Mama or Daddy, or sometimes with Gramma. She never picks a fight with Grampa, because you can't hardly pick a fight with Grampa. Gramma says he's impossible to fight with, which makes him especially irritating. She says Grampa always gets his way because he's always happy no matter what happens. Gramma says a person like that can drive another person crazy.

Daddy is telling Granny that she doesn't have to do this, that the cemetery workers will take care of it. She snorts at him and says if he believes that, he's a bigger fool than she thinks he is. I think this is the same fight they have every time we go visit our dead. Their fight ranges beyond our dead and into things I don't understand, like how Daddy doesn't need to see that other woman and that he ought to stay home and be happy and keep himself out of trouble for once.

Outside the gates of Assumption Cemetery, Daddy stops long enough to get the red wagon out of the trunk and puts both Granny's bags in it: the one she never leaves the house without and the one with her gardening tools. We head out on the path that leads through the cemetery. It's a hike from the gates to the old part of the cemetery, where our people are.

Granny has a lot of dead. They all died before I was ever born, but I feel like I know them because of all the visits. It makes Granny sad to come here, and when she's sad, she tells me stories. Grandpa Arthur, Uncle Eloi, Aunt Leoni who was carried off by the measles when she was younger than me, Aunt Aletha and her husband whose name we never say are all buried here. Mama doesn't like me to come with Granny, but she can't visit by herself, and besides, I don't mind. Mama never comes to visit her dead babies, and always says, "Let the dead bury the dead," which doesn't make any sense to me. She also claims that Daddy's relatives die spectacularly, not like her family, who all just fade away.

Granny gets upset every time we come, because Aunt Aletha is buried with her husband's people and not with ours. I'm not supposed to know about what happened to them, but I heard Mama and Granny talking about it one time. Aunt Aletha was very beautiful and married rich. She and her husband flew airplanes and went on hunting trips and drove fast cars. Granny always says I'd look just like Aletha if I weren't so homely. But Aunt Aletha decided she didn't want to be married anymore. When she told her husband she was leaving, he shot her and then killed himself because he didn't want to live without her. They both got buried with his people, because his family was determined to hush it all up, and it would look bad if she got buried somewhere else.

Between the wars, Uncle Eloi and Daddy went off to work the pipeline on their own for the first time, in the dark. Uncle Eloi died when some pipe fell on him and crushed him. Grandpa Arthur's heart was broken, and he took to his bed and died of grief. The last thing he said to Daddy was, "It should have been you." My daddy was fifteen, and he was the man of the family.

Granny only has Daddy and Aunt Odilia left, plus the rest of us, but we don't count so much.

The stone path through the cemetery is winding and sometimes hard to follow because it is broken up, and the wagon lurches along. Moss drips from ancient oak trees, and whole limbs touch the ground. It is crowded, and all the graves are above ground. Rich families bury their people in little stone houses with their name over the door and coffins stacked on shelves inside. People like us have concrete vaults that the coffins go inside. Poor people get put in the walls, and their bones swept back for the next person. Our family vault has a little iron fence around it, which is rusting because of the weather here. Inside the fence is a little patch of grass that goes all around the vault. On the side of the vault are small metal plaques with the names of everybody buried inside.

Our job is to tidy everything up. We weed and trim the grass with shears from Granny's bag and polish the metal plaque so all the names are clear. We pick up the fallen gray moss and wash off and brush the tomb clean of the fresh green moss that grows everywhere. We pick up broken pieces of concrete and stone and try to put them back where they belong as best we can. Sometimes, we bring fresh flowers and take away dead ones. Everything in Louisiana rusts or mildews, or both at the same time. This part of the cemetery seems like a little town, with our family surrounded by neighbors. I like to think of them that way, and not as all alone.

When we have finished tidying up, Granny just likes to sit with her family for a while. If she's in the mood, she tells me stories. We spread an old quilt on the bench across the lane from our family vault and make ourselves comfortable. If she doesn't feel like talking, she closes her eyes and pretends to sleep, but I know she is remembering. Remembering a boy who looked like Daddy but shorter, and a girl who looked like me but pretty. Sometimes I try to think about what it would be like to be Granny, with most of my family dead. I think it must explain why she is so mean sometimes.

When she doesn't want to talk, I go for a walk to the oldest part of the cemetery. There, almost every tomb and vault is broken, and nobody visits much anymore. I like to visit these people everybody else has forgotten. I read the names and dates, though some of the names are so old or covered in moss that you can't read them anymore. I like to look for a boy or girl my same age, so I can imagine what their lives were like. It used to be that lots of kids died, so it's not hard to find somebody. Sometimes I make up stories about them, and sometimes I just tell them about my life, and about stuff like cars and airplanes and outer space or the movie I just saw.

When Granny's ready, we go see Aunt Aletha. This is the hardest part for her. We can't really do anything at the mausoleum, because it is always spotless and it isn't ours. Granny never stays here long, because she doesn't like the people Aunt Aletha is buried with. She says that they were ugly to Aletha when she was alive, and that she shouldn't have to spend all eternity with them. Plus, that awful boy who shot her shouldn't get to keep her. But it is too late to do anything about it now. So, we just stand for a few minutes, Granny with her hand on Aunt Aletha's name, and me with the red wagon.

We meet up with Daddy back at the gate. He's careful that he's never late, and is always waiting for us. He loads up the red wagon and the supplies and the trash and his mother. Sometimes, on the way home, we stop for dinner along the way, but most times, Granny is too sad, so we just drive straight home, and she goes to bed. Daddy says if it makes her so sad, why doesn't she just quit visiting. She gets real mad at him then and says she has reason to remember them, even if he doesn't. I sit in the back and try not to listen to them fight. When they do, I know that soon, Granny will be gone to Aunt Odilia in the north. My family is good at going away.

CHAPTER TEN

☙ ☙

1960 — Storm

"WAKE UP." She shakes me a little too hard. "Wake up. Get up." I struggle up from the warm darkness of sleep, trying to break the surface of awareness. She urges frantically, "Put this on. Take this. Come on. We have to get the boys."

It's my mama, and something's wrong. I try to do what she asks, but I am clumsy with sleep and stumble as I follow her to the boys' room, dragging blanket and robe and some book she's handed me.

Outside, the wind wails, thunder booms, rain lashes, and lightning makes it bright as day. I understand now: a storm. My mama hates storms. That's not quite right. My mama is afraid of storms, deathly afraid.

I hurry to catch up down the long hall. She's already there, pulling Henry David out of the top bunk and standing him against the wall. He's the hardest to wake up, but he'll follow you around like a sleepwalker doing what he's told. Samuel Taylor wakes up scared, crying. Mama's reassuring him everything's all right, but he's not having it. She hands me Oscar Fingal, the baby, who's been sleeping soundly on her hip, picks up Samuel Taylor, and grabs Henry David's hand.

We head back down the hallway and into the living room, where there's a huge picture window that faces out onto the yard. From here, it looks like we live in the country; you can't tell we have neighbors. The yard slopes down to a creek lined by trees and bushes. The sky goes on forever.

Next to the fireplace, which we never use because Granny's convinced that somebody will get burned to death, is Mama's rocker. She piles the little ones in on her lap, blankets and robes and boys, covers all, and settles in. I take my place on the wide arm, and she hands me the flashlight from somewhere. That's my job, to hold the flashlight. She probably has another one tucked away somewhere in case we need it.

Outside, the storm builds, raging against the window. Branches blow by, and patio furniture gets overturned. The storm is loud, but Mama is louder. "What should I sing first?" she asks brightly, as if it wasn't the middle of the night, as if we all weren't terrified. "How about 'The Little Old Ford'?" She launches into it without waiting for anybody to reply. Henry David is still half asleep, Samuel Taylor's still sniveling, and Oscar Fingal has found his foot and is perfectly happy.

Now Henry Jones and a pretty little queen
took a ride one day in his big limousine.
The car kicked up and the engine wouldn't crank
there wasn't any gas in the gasoline tank.
Just about that time, along came Nord
and he rambled right along in his little old Ford.

The song goes on forever. Mama sings loudly and tune-lessly over the storm. Gramma despairs that the musi-cal talent in our family seems to have stopped with her. Henry David rouses by the third verse, which is his favorite. Mama rocks furiously in time to the music, or the storm. She is holding everybody too tight, and they squirm to get comfortable.

Mama has been afraid of storms as long as I can remem-ber. Sometimes she builds a blanket fort over the dining room table and fills it with pillows, and we slip inside to a place where nothing outside can find us. I get sent out for snacks, and bring back potato chips and a pitcher of Kool-Aid and some Dixie cups. She is especially scared when Daddy isn't home.

Tonight is not a blanket fort night. It is a rocking chair night. While I listen to Mama and the boys, I watch the storm outside. I am not afraid. If it was up to me, I'd stand outside in the big middle of it. I'd get soaked with rain, and the wind would blow my hair and nightgown and I would never, ever come inside. I would let the lightning strike me, and I would glow in the dark. The storm would blow me away from this house and these people and set me down somewhere else, and I would be someone brand new.

But Mama's fear keeps me inside, and I will never be anywhere but here, and anyone but me. Mama elbows me and asks me if I've fallen asleep.

"Your turn," she says. I recite "Little Willie," which is Grampa's favorite poem, and because it's the only thing I can remember right now.

> *Little Willie in the best of sashes*
> *Fell in the fire and was burnt to ashes.*
> *By and by the room grew chilly*
> *But no one wanted to poke up Willie.*

CHAPTER ELEVEN

❧ ❧

1961 — *Bedroom Door*

THEY'RE A SOLEMN GROUP, my little brothers, gathered around my parents' bedroom door.

"Mama's not up yet," says Henry David, always optimistic. Since he started talking, he hardly ever shuts up. This morning, he is hopeful.

"She's not getting up," croaks Samuel Taylor, always pessimistic.

"What are we doing about breakfast?" demands pragmatist Oscar Fingal.

"Cheewios," chortles baby GeorgG Gordon.

I decide to go with GeorgG's plan, since it is the only one we've got, and herd the boys, half sullen, half excited, down the hall to the kitchen. We sleep on the other end of the house in three bedrooms, and our parents sleep on this end. In between are the living room, family room, dining room, and kitchen.

I install the boys at the kitchen counter, praying this is not the morning that GeorgG follows our cousin Amy to heaven by falling off the stool and breaking his head open. He sits between the two oldest boys, Henry David and Samuel Taylor, who will keep their eyes on him. Finn sits at the end, ready to run errands.

I use a stool to get down five Tupperware bowls and their matching cups, each set a different color. Mine are pink, Henry David's blue, Samuel Taylor's green, Oscar Fingal's yellow, and GeorgG's orange.

From the pantry, I pull the large box of Cheerios, and carefully pour the right amount into each bowl. From the refrigerator, I take both milk and orange juice. The gallon jug is almost too heavy for me to carry. I half-fill the cups with juice, except for GeorgG's, which I half-fill with milk. Carefully, I pour milk on the cereal, except for GeorgG's, because he would rather eat it dry with his hands, and this morning, I don't want to teach him the importance of good table manners. I don't put milk on mine, either, because it'll be soggy before I get a chance to eat it. I promise the boys that after everybody's finished eating and all the bowls and cups are in the sink, they can watch cartoons on the TV in the family room. I am glad it's not a school day, so I don't have to get everybody ready and off and try and figure out what to do with the baby.

"You watch him," I sternly remind Hank and Sam as I start down the hall to Mama's room, wondering just how bad things are. The boys prefer their recently-chosen nick-names; at home, everyone uses their double names. Daddy's in Arkansas, Gramma and Grampa are in Georgia, and Granny's in Michigan. The people around here don't know that Mama sometimes has bad days, and we're not supposed to tell.

What am I going to do if it's a really bad day?

I stand outside the bedroom door, wondering just how bad this day is.

I knock, but there's no answer. I knock again, louder; still no answer. I am not supposed to go in if there's no answer. I am supposed to find the nearest adult and let them figure out what to do. But I don't have a nearest adult and we don't talk to strangers, so I take a deep breath and try the doorknob, hoping it isn't locked. It isn't. The room is dark and stuffy. Only a sliver of light sneaks through the drawn curtains, and dust motes dance in it. Grampa used to tell me the dust was fairies, but Gramma told me the truth. Gramma tells the truth a lot, even when it isn't the best story. I close the door behind me.

I can see Mama in the bed, buried below a mound of covers. It looks like she's built herself a fort to keep the world away. I wonder what it's like in there. I call "Mama," to let her know I'm in the room. She doesn't answer. I didn't really think she would.

I cross the room. I know she can't hear me coming, because the carpet is so deep and swallows up all the sound my bare feet might make. So it doesn't seem like I'm sneaking up on her, I keep talking softly as I move toward the bed. I can hear my heart pounding. I am afraid of what I might find.

"I got the boys fed, Mama. Cheerios. They're gonna watch TV now. We'll all read after that, I promise." Mama doesn't much like cartoons, but I think they have their place. Like now. Especially now.

I stand by the bed now and try to figure out exactly where her head is. It's awful dark in here, and I can't tell for sure if the covers are moving up and down. My chest is tight and my mouth is dry. What if...

But no, there's a soft moan from the bed. "DG?"

"Yes, Mama?"

"Headache, DG. All night. Still bad."

I breathe a great big old sigh of relief, and my chest loosens up. I know what to do for a headache. Mama's been getting migraines my whole life. I could write a book about headaches.

I go over and twitch the curtains to shut out the last of the light. Then I go into the bathroom and wet a washrag with cool water for the back of her neck. I get up on the vanity so that I can reach her headache pills, which are kept on a high, high shelf so nobody takes them accidentally. Even before I could read, I knew exactly how many pills to help her take and how often.

Mama's headaches are pretty awful. She can't stand light or noise or food or anything when she has one. The good thing is they mostly only last a day or so. When they last longer, she has to go the hospital. Not the away hospital, but the one where she gets to come home the same day. If the headache lasts too long, Mama has to go away. If she can talk to me now, she'll probably be better tonight or tomorrow. Before I leave, I tell her not to worry about us, we'll be fine.

I head out to the family room, where the boys are arguing over what to watch next. I don't like cartoons, so I don't care what they watch, but Mama usually reads to us on Saturday morning. I turn off the TV and gather everybody into Mama's big rocker that looks out through the wall-size picture window and over the back lawn to the woods beyond. This view is very different in daylight, not at all scary like it is at night. Mama has been reading *Oliver Twist* to us at night, but I can't do all the voices, so I have to choose something else.

"Sing, DG, sing," requests Finn. Usually, singing is for stormy nights, but since today is kind of like a stormy night, I agree. I don't sing very well, but I remember all the words. I like dramatic songs that let you do a little acting. Gramma favors Protestant hymns, since she's played them every Wednesday night and Sunday morning for about a hundred years. Mama likes musical comedies from Broadway, which is all the way in New York City. She learns about them on Ed Sullivan's show or from movies. Grampa loves old parlor songs that were popular when he was a boy. Daddy likes country and western and rockabilly, but he'll pretty much listen to anything. Granny likes old country music that you can dance to, though I've never seen her dance.

Hank and Sammy sing together on "Nadine" and "Maybelline," which are two of my daddy's favorites. Finn sings "Whispering Hope," which, to Gramma's dismay, is the only thing all of us can play on the piano. GeorgG sings "Old MacDonald," because that's the only song he's learned so far, and it goes on forever. When it gets to be my turn, I choose "The Wild Side of Life" and "Honkytonk Angel." I've never been in a honkytonk, but I like to imagine the dark and the smoke and sound of unidentifiable stuff crunching on the floor. And the music and the dancing, especially those. I think honkytonks must be the most romantic places in the world. When I get old enough to date, I am only going out with boys who take me to honkytonks.

Since it is getting near lunchtime, I choose for my last song "Saturday Night in a Barroom," which is one of the most dramatic songs Mama ever sings. She puts a lot of *umph* into it that even Porter Wagoner, who made a record of it, didn't manage. He could learn stuff about drama from Mama, who used to act when she was younger. But Mama's still not here, so I do the best I can, singing where it's called for and then dropping into a speaking voice that's almost a whisper toward the end. If you're standing up, you can do gestures and everything, but since we're rocking away, I make do with just my voice. The boys are suitably silent after that, and peer around like they think Jesus might appear and mark the fall of a sparrow right here in our family room.

For lunch, we have cold wienies and hot dog buns, since I'm not allowed to use the oven or the stove without supervision. Our family is prone to cooking fires. Gramma says it's 'cause we're so distractable. I can use the toaster, but I don't think the wienies will fit, and the hot dog buns sure don't. Hank and Sammy argue about just what they should call this lunch, and Finn tells them they don't have to call it anything, because nobody's asking.

While the boys are eating, I go check on Mama to see if she needs more medicine or anything else I can get her. She's still buried in darkness, but asks for and drinks a whole glass of water. I get her one more pill from the bathroom and bump my shin on the way down. She'll kiss the bruise when she feels better.

"Get two dollars from my purse. Take the boys to Miss Mamie's and buy them ice cream. I'll be up for supper. You can take the truck. Stay inside the fence the whole way. Don't even think about getting on the road."

I can tell she feels a whole lot better, and maybe she will be up for supper. I never get to take the truck out on my own. Usually Daddy or Red, the hired man, ride with me. I feel very grown up.

I round up the boys and tell them about the ice cream, which gets everybody in their clothes without an argument, though Finn will only wear his too-small Superman costume from last Halloween, and GeorgG won't wear shoes, just socks. Once everybody is decent enough to take out in public, I put on a nice dress and my new shoes and put Mama's two dollars in my Sunday purse, which is more money than has ever been in there at one time.

I get everybody loaded into the back of the truck and off we go to Miss Mamie's, which is at the corner of our property line and the county road. I drive very slowly and very carefully. The only advantage to being as tall as I am, is that with the seat pulled all the way up and a pillow behind my back, I can reach the pedals just fine. When we get there, the boys pile out all covered in hay, which Miss Mamie won't mind, since we have cash money in hand. It sure is hard to keep boys clean. I carry GeorgG, while Hank holds Finn with one hand and Sammy with the other, and look both ways before we cross the road.

There is much discussion about which ice cream treat to buy, since Miss Mamie's is almost as good as an ice cream truck for choice. I am afraid Sammy's will melt before Finn decides. GeorgG just wants whatever everybody else is having, and since they can't decide, he's getting fretful the way he always does when there's a disagreement. I finally tell them that if they don't decide, everybody is getting a vanilla Dixie cup, which is hardly a treat at all. Everybody makes a grab for their favorite, and GeorgG gets a Rainbow Pushup, which I will have to wash off him and his clothes later. Miss Mamie tells us not to open our ice creams till we get out of the store, so we sit on the bench out front swinging our legs, and everybody and their ice cream melting in the heat. Before I take the boys back across the county road to the truck parked in our pasture, I use Miss Mamie's hose to rinse the worst of the mess off.

I load them back up in the back of the truck, with the usual warnings about keeping their hands inside and everybody sitting down the whole time and no horsing around. They mostly listen to me. They are pretty good for boys, especially when Mama is sick for a day. It is only when she is gone for a long time that we forget to be good. Or when she is here for a long time and not sick. We get loud and rowdy, and fight all the time over stupid stuff. I drive back across the pasture, wondering why people ever have kids. I don't think I ever will. Our house looms in the distance.

I sometimes wonder if having all us kids is part of what makes Mama sick. We're a lot to deal with, and it wears her out. She has to take care of us whether or not she feels like it. I know she gets real sad thinking about all the babies that didn't live, almost as many of them as there are of us. It bothers her when Daddy is away so much, working all the time. He works until late at night, even when the other men are already home. He says he doesn't want to be away, but he goes anyway, and sometimes he stays for a long time. Mama tries to understand, but it seems like she gets smaller and smaller and quieter and quieter, until she just disappears to the special hospital.

When she comes back, it is always a little strange. Daddy is here all the time and being extra charming. Mama has to ease back into being home, and everybody treats her like she's made of glass. She forgets stuff, too, like which is sugar and which is salt, and that you don't have spaghetti for breakfast. And sometimes, birthdays. If they don't get her medicine right, she stays up all night and sleeps all day, or she loses too much weight or gets too fat. It is hard to know what to expect.

We try not to talk about her being sick outside the family. A lot of people don't understand that having a mental illness is just like any other kind of sickness. They treat Mama like she might strip off all her clothes and climb the big oak tree by the county courthouse. She doesn't do stuff like that, except for that one time when she got afraid that we might all be dead and came to school in her nightgown looking for us so she'd know we were all right.

I know some kids can't come to our house, because their mothers are worried something might happen. We keep mostly to ourselves. We'll probably move soon, anyway. Daddy doesn't like to stay too long in one place. But that doesn't matter today, because today she just has a headache, and a headache will go away. Then everything will be fine again.

CHAPTER TWELVE

⊷ ⊷

1961 — *Farmers*

IT HAS BEEN A HARD YEAR. Daddy retired and moved us to this farm in north Louisiana, then he got bored and went back to work and just left us here in the middle of nowhere. Gramma and Grampa live far away now, in Georgia, but I write Grampa long letters that I take out behind the barn and burn, which I mustn't do anymore, since it almost caught fire last time. Henry David lost the sight in one eye when he got hit with a rock on the playground at school, but he won't be like Uncle Lee with a glass eye. Just his regular eye that doesn't work anymore. Mama lost another baby and was away again for a while. Everybody is just sad all the time, and I don't know how to fix it.

None of us fit here. Daddy's dream of living on a farm is just that—Daddy's dream. We try, but I don't think we're really farm people. Only Granny loves it here. She has chickens and rabbits and pigs, and a garden so big she needs help with it. We spend all our time trying not to get bit by animals. What I have learned so far: chickens are vicious, and animals run away if you even think about leaving a door or a gate open. Somebody left a pasture gate open the other day, and cows escaped onto the highway, and now we have more beef to eat than we know what to do with. I didn't even know you could get tired of steak. Bacon does not taste as good if you know its name. I would become a vegetarian if I liked vegetables. I don't think you can live on just potatoes and carrots.

I think the people in this town are mean. The kids at school tease us about everything, from our clothes to the way we talk. Mama and Daddy get up every morning at five o'clock to make coffee and fresh biscuits and gravy, because the farmers come over to visit as soon as they finish their chores. They caught Mama and Daddy still asleep in bed a couple of times and made fun of them, and now they both get up, get ready, and nap on the couch in case somebody stops by. People just let themselves in the kitchen door. Mama says we ought to lock it, but Daddy says we can't do that, because people will think we're unfriendly.

Somebody sold Daddy a horse so us kids could learn to ride. Her name is Scooter, and that should have told him all he needed to know. She is twenty-six years old and sixteen hands high, whatever that means. The man who sold her to Daddy bragged about how gentle she was and how she was the perfect horse for kids to learn to ride on. She's fine until she gets tired, then she runs flat out for the barn and looks for the nearest place she can run under and "scoot" you off her back. If you're lucky, it is the shed near the barn. If you're not, she scrapes you off using a tree limb, and then you have to walk miles to get home, if nobody notices she's back and comes to look for you first.

Mama hates the chickens, so I get to go out and feed them before I go school and again before we have supper, which is a bad idea, since the chickens hate me. No matter what the weather is, I've got to bundle up so they don't peck me to death. I wear Granny's rubber boots, oven mitts on both hands, and a scarf around my neck. I'm lucky that I already wear glasses, or I'd probably be blind by now. First, I get the chicken feed in a big bucket, and then drag it over to where the chickens live. They have a pen with a yard and a house in the pen, but it doesn't make them any nicer. Chickens are just not very appreciative. Once you get the feed to the pen, you need to real fast open the gate, get the bucket inside, and get the gate shut and locked behind you, which is not very easy when you are wearing oven mitts. If you don't, there will be chickens all over the backyard, and they are very difficult to herd back into their pen. If you do manage to get in without letting any of them out, you get swarmed by starving chickens. They start pecking all over you, which is why I wear the boots and gloves. I've seen the scars on Mama's ankles from where the chickens got her when she was a little girl. Granny calls us a bunch of sissies and sends me out anyway, no matter how much I beg and offer to do other chores instead for the rest of my life. I am trying to teach myself how to throw up, so I can pretend to be sick and maybe avoid chicken duty all together.

The bigger boys, Henry David and Samuel Taylor, help with the pig feeding, which is even more dangerous than chicken feeding, since pigs will actually eat little boys. Red told us all about how the little boy on the last farm he worked at got eaten by the pigs when he leaned too far out over the fence and fell in the pigpen, where he may or may not have drowned in the mud before the pigs ate him up. Red likes to tell this story over and over, but never in front of Mama and Daddy, and he always changes his mind about the boy and the mud. Either way, pig feeding is dangerous, and oven mitts are no help at all. Every time we eat, the boys help Granny put all the food scraps in an old pickle bucket out in the mudroom. Granny says this is what makes the pork taste so good. The boys drag that bucket out when it gets full, and tip it into the pig trough. Usually, Granny makes them strip down in the yard after, and washes them down with the hose before she lets them back in, because they get more scraps on them than in the trough.

I don't know why Daddy would bring us to a place where we could die at any minute. I don't know why anyone would want to live in the country. There is not even a library in this town except the school library, and I've read all the books they have for elementary kids, and the librarian won't let me check out any other books unless my mama goes to the school board for permission. Mama says, "Can we just not? They think we are strange enough already." She promises to take me to the library in Mer Rouge at least once a month, so I say okay. She's also joining the Book of the Month Club and ordering *Reader's Digest* Condensed Books, because Granny likes those a lot—those and religious books. Granny's losing her regular religion in her old age. She's stopped going to mass, and reads the Bible all the time. I don't have any friends at school, because I'm a grade ahead in reading and a grade below in arithmetic, and I go to different classes for those subjects. The kids make fun of me for that, and I don't get to know anybody very well, because I'm always moving around the school. It is embarrassing to be so stupid with numbers. It means I work with kids who have been held back, like dumb old RubyDeen, who nobody likes.

On Saturdays, we go into town to run errands and to shake and howdy. I don't always get to go, because sometimes the boys need haircuts, and I'm not allowed in the barbershop. If I am with them, Daddy gives me a dollar and I get to go to the five and dime to shop. I am also not allowed in the pool hall, which means the two most interesting places in town are off limits. Granny says that if I am alone, I must always cross the street to avoid passing directly in front of them. Last Saturday, I almost got run over trying to avoid them. If Mama is with us, she and I go to the Woolworth's and sit at the counter and have cherry or vanilla cokes. Sometimes we go to the dress shop, where Missus Wilson lets me try on hats and Mama looks at shoes. We don't buy much here, maybe just school clothes, because we go to New Orleans or Memphis to shop for real clothes.

Sometimes, I ignore Granny and just walk on by, because the five and dime is only two doors down from the barber shop and I'd have to cross over, then cross again and circle back, and could just end up smashed flat in the middle of Main Street by some farmer not expecting a jaywalker. It doesn't much matter if I do pass by accidentally, because you can't hardly see anything anyway, just a bunch of men talking, playing dominoes, and reading magazines and smoking and waiting to get their hair cut—or just waiting on their wives to finish whatever they're doing, which in this town is next to nothing.

I don't know what Daddy was expecting when he moved us here, but I don't think he got it. I know that the real farmers laugh at him behind his back. I think he knows it, too. Now he doesn't spend much time at home unless he has too. We've been here nearly a year, and it isn't getting much better. Daddy's decided to throw a big party and invite everybody in town and some of the pipeliners he knows from around the area. I invite all the girls from my homeroom, including RubyDeen. They don't even like me, but Mama says I still have to invite them.

Pipeliners hardly ever live in cities. Since they always work away, they can live in the middle of nowhere. Since they travel around so much, they like to have a home place near family if they can. We don't have much family to live near, but Daddy says we are all we need. If that's true, I don't know why we have to have this party. It's a lot of work for everybody, especially Mama. She and Granny are cooking everything but the meat, which Daddy will cook on great big grills, and even a goat in a pit. Other people will bring a covered dish, which means a lot of green bean salad and Jello salad, which is just Jello with strange stuff in it, which is a waste of good Jello, if you ask me. Mama will make her famous ambrosia, which I guess isn't famous here.

Daddy had Red dig another pit for a fire so they can boil water for crawfish, which I will never understand, since they look like bugs to me. People in Louisiana just go crazy over them. At least they are cooking them outside, so I don't have to do much to avoid them. Daddy just gets mad when he thinks about my allergies.

There's a tent set up out in the front yard to the side of the house. Old folks and babies hang out there to nap. All the kids keep asking if we really have an alligator in the pond, and I just tell them, "Yes, we do. Don't get too close, or you'll be part of the barbecue!" I think one of the boys must have told that whopper, but I'm not giving him away. We are exactly the kind of people who could have an alligator if we wanted.

More and more people show up, spreading quilts and lawn chairs across the grass. Cars and trucks of every kind pile up in parking jumbles along the wide driveway to the house. Everybody's more or less sweaty, with the little boys on the seriously sweaty end of the scale, and older ladies on the just dewy end.

The men all gather around the various cooking pots and grills, lending their advice and starting arguments over sauce or no sauce, and spitting into the fires. They drink beer to stay cool, while the ladies sip sweet tea and the kids drink lemonade as fast as the teenagers can squeeze lemons.

The afternoon feels strange, disconnected, out of time somehow. There is no set time for anything. People wander up to a long line of picnic tables covered in red-and-white checked tablecloths and fill a paper plate with food, then wander off to eat. The desserts fill one table, and sometimes people start with them before they've even had their dinner. If the potato salad or a casserole runs empty, there's always another one in the kitchen to replace it. It is supposed to be my job to keep an eye on things, but I only remember to check once in a while. The food magically replenishes itself without me.

When people aren't eating, there's croquet, horseshoes, and badminton set up. Somebody has dragged a couple of card tables from somewhere, and people play pinochle or canasta or other games. Old men play dominoes in the shade. Kids dart in and out of everywhere, trailing dragonflies and warnings behind them. Mothers and fathers lazily call out, "Don't run around so much in this heat; you'll make yourself sick," or "Settle down; it wears me out to watch you," but they don't get up and chase after them.

The afternoon becomes sluggish, with children and adults slowing down as they fill up on food and drinks and the humidity. Babies begin to nap, scattered across laps and quilts and the grass like they've fallen under a spell.

I need go to the bathroom, so I detach myself from the of the gaggle of little girls sitting under a tree near the pond, talking about boys and summer plans and movie stars. RubyDeen follows me as she has all day, still disbelieving her good fortune at being invited to this party. RubyDeen is the least-liked girl in our whole school, but Mama made me invite *all* the girls, so here she is. RubyDeen thinks this makes her my new best friend, but it doesn't. She has dirty blonde hair and a dirty neck, and her clothes aren't cute, and she's not very smart. She doesn't like to read and can't hardly anyway. Mama says I should be extra nice to RubyDeen because she doesn't have the same advantages as the rest of us, but it is really hard to be nice to someone who smells.

The house is dark and cool and quiet compared to the yard. I head toward the bathroom with RubyDeen on my heels, gawking at everything she sees on the way. I wonder if her family even has indoor plumbing. This is the bathroom I share with the boys, and it is divided up into three rooms: one for the sinks, one for the toilet, and one for the bathtub. Mama says that way, we can get maximum use out of it, because three, even four of us can be in there at once with all the doors closed. I shut myself in the toilet and take care of my business, leaving RubyDeen to wander around the rest of the bathroom. When I come out to wash my hands, RubyDeen is standing there with big eyes and a funny look on her face.

"What?" I ask her, checking to see if I am dragging toilet paper on one foot or if my clothes are twisted funny.

She grabs my unwashed hand and pulls me out of the bathroom, farther down the hall, deeper into the house. Our feet make no sound on the carpet, but I can hear noises now. Whimpering and a kind of knocking. At the doorway to my bedroom, RubyDeen stops and points with her free hand.

A man and woman, all tangled up, are leaning against the closet door, which is making the knocking sound as they move against it. The woman makes the whimpers. Her face is buried in the man's chest, so I cannot see who she is. I would recognize the man anywhere.

I pull RubyDeen away from the door and we run back down the hallway, out of house as fast as we can. We reach the patio and I am still holding RubyDeen's hand as I see my mother and Mr. Burris, a friend of my daddy's, coming toward the house. My mouth is dry and my eyes are wet. Mama hails us. "You girls see anyone in the house? Burris is looking for Lena."

RubyDeen's hand tightens in mine, and we look at each other. I look back at Mama and my mouth moves, but nothing comes out. RubyDeen squeezes my hand again and says, "No, ma'am. Just us. You sure got a fancy bathroom."

Mama laughs in agreement. "Yes, we do, Ruby. Come on, Burris. Let's check the kitchen for that knife you want."

Before I can think of anything to say, the door behind us squeaks open. We all turn slightly to see Miss Lena, smoothing her dress down over its petticoats, and Daddy stepping down onto the patio. Everyone freezes for a moment.

"You girls better run along and play now." Mr. Burris's voice is deep and very sharp, like the knife he is looking for. RubyDeen pulls on me and we slowly move to the edge of the patio. Something will happen when we leave, and that thought frightens me.

I stop, digging in my heels to hold RubyDeen in place. "Mama?"

My mother's face is white against her dark hair. I can't read the expression on her face. She just says, "Go," and we do, RubyDeen pulling me along behind her, dodging tables and pets and little boys running around.

We don't stop until we reach the far side of the small pond. We fall into the grass on our backs, breathing heavily and staring at the sky, still clutching hands. RubyDeen turns her head toward me. "I won't never tell nobody. Never," she swears, as tears roll into my ears. I can hear the words of that song as I lie here. *I've got tears in my ears from lyin' on my back, in my bed while I cry over you....*

I sit up when the noise reaches us across the pond. Up the gentle slope of the hill toward the house, people are stirring to see what the commotion is. I see my mama with her arms clasped tightly around herself. Miss Lena has her head down and isn't looking at anybody. Mr. Burris and my daddy look squared up to fight, and some of the other men move in as if to stop it. My daddy is laughing and smiling as if he thinks something is funny.

After a standoff during which men hold Mr. Burris back, the not-fight is over. Mr. Burris grabs Miss Lena by the arm and drags her to the car. Others follow as the party breaks up. I watch my mother hand out wax paper and aluminum foil for leftovers, and act like nothing is wrong.

RubyDeen is still sitting beside me. "It don't matter. What he did. Won't nobody at school know anyway. It's not on you. It's on him. He ain't bad as some." She pauses, and I wonder what her daddy is like. I have never met him. Fathers don't usually come to school.

After a minute, she continues, "It's a real nice party. I think most ever'body had a real good time. I enjoyed myself. Thank you for inviting me." The last part comes out funny, like she practiced it over and over. I ask RubyDeen to spend the night, and we call her parents for permission. She will wear my pajamas and borrow clothes for tomorrow. I tell my mother what I have done, and she looks at me with dull eyes. RubyDeen and I help in the kitchen to get all the extra dishes washed and put away. We get the boys ready for bed. RubyDeen mops the kitchen floor. She says she is used to housework.

At the door to my bedroom, I balk. I don't want to sleep here; anywhere else will do. But RubyDeen takes my hand, leads me inside, and closes the door behind us.

In the morning, RubyDeen's daddy takes her away in a rusty pickup truck with a mess of dogs and boys in the back. She wears a pretty summer dress that is too short for me, and her hair is brushed and shiny. Mama has braided it with ribbons. She waves at me as they drive away. I watch until the truck is out of sight.

A month later, Daddy moves us to Georgia, where he promises everything will be different. But Mama goes away again.

CHAPTER THIRTEEN

᭡ ᭡

1962 — *Holy Card*

SHE'S JUST BACK ONE DAY when I get home from school. Banging in the front door, I drop my books and head toward the kitchen. It smells like somebody's been baking, and since there isn't a fire truck out front, I guess it isn't Gramma.

I've got something to brag about for a change, because I got a Holy Card for knowing something that Mary Catherine Moynaghan didn't. I slam around the corner fast as I dare, because it's burning a hole in my pocket, and I don't want to take the chance of losing it before anybody gets to see it and everybody starts thinking I'm telling whoppers again.

At the kitchen sink, my mama stands with her back to me. Her hair's a dark cloud against the white lace of the kitchen curtains. *My mama's home.* She's been gone exactly twenty-nine days this time. I mark each one on the calendar I keep under my bed.

I skid to a stop, then hurl myself at her, crying, "Mama!" She sways forward, leans into the counter, and makes a little *oomph* sound, like I've knocked all the air out of her. I'm holding on real tight around her waist, and I can't hardly breathe for crying.

She stiffens just for a second and it feels like she might run away, so I hold on tighter, and for the first time since she went away, I'm crying, really crying, afraid I might make her go away again. I'm hiccuping and I need to blow my nose awful, and if I keep this up, I'm going to need that inhaler I traded to Danny Boyle for a banana that wasn't brown and mushy.

Mama's hands move to press my arms away, and I'm so afraid I'll lose her. She loosens my grip a little, turns in the circle of my arms, puts her hands on my head like a blessing, and just lets me be.

When she finally speaks, she sounds far away. "I'd forgotten how bright your hair is." Her voice is very low, and scratchier than I remember.

She lets me cry and hold her, swaying just a little while I sob. She feels so warm, and smells just like her closet. After a while, she slips to her knees, presses her forehead against mine, and wipes gently at the tears and snot that cover my face.

This close, I can see everything—her skin softer and paler than any doll's, her big eyes with impossibly long lashes and thumbprint-dark shadows underneath and little lines in the corners, and on her right temple, there's a red mark, like a burn, the size of a quarter, that fades into her hair.

She pulls back a bit and stares at me real hard, trying to tame my wild hair a little with her soft hand. Her other hand slips under my chin and tilts my face up a little, and then her voice, still far away, asks me, "Which one? Which one of my children are you?"

Gramma, who's been real still and quiet all this time, explodes across the kitchen like a chicken out of a henhouse. "Now, Margaret, you know this girl. You've only got the one. Easy to tell her from the boys. This is DG."

Mama's standing now, swaying a little—but me, I'm still as a statue, and hoping I don't throw up on Gramma's clean kitchen floor. It feels like somebody's kicked me in the stomach. I can't breathe. *My mama doesn't know me.* It's never been *this* bad before. My world turns upside down while Gramma scoots me to the table, hands me milk and cookies that aren't store-bought or burnt, and flutters around the kitchen, muttering.

My mama, wearing a lavender sweater that matches the shadows under her eyes, stands swaying in the middle of the kitchen.

Grampa's there, too, must have been there the whole time, and I realize that I musta sailed right by him in my excitement to share my good news. He walks toward my mama with his hand out while she says "Papa," in a sort of half question.

"Oh, Pegeen," he says, "come with me. We'll sit out on the gallery, and I'll tell you all about this girl. I know all her best secrets." He winks at me, and his voice wraps around her like a blanket. That's his best voice, the one with music in it, the one he uses for stories, the one he usually saves for me. She takes his hand, and they walk out of the kitchen toward the front of the house.

My cookies are cold, and my milk is warm, but it doesn't much matter, because I couldn't swallow them around this lump in my throat, anyway.

"Come dry dishes, you'll feel better," Gramma commands. I don't understand how drying dishes is going to help me feel better, but I hope this is one of the times my grownups are right about something.

"Do you have questions, DG?" She hands me down a dish, and a cloth to dry it with.

I am the girl whose mother doesn't know her name. I have no questions.

Gramma's still looking at me, waiting for an answer.

"No, ma'm."

Then she's bustling out of the kitchen. "Your mama, she's just tired. She'll be herself in a little while. She just needs to rest up, eat some good food, get back to her life. She'll be fine. You'll see, she'll be just fine."

I sit down at the table and tell the empty kitchen, "I got a Holy Card today. For being smart and for being quiet about it. You want to see?"

CHAPTER FOURTEEN

⇝ ⇝

1963 — Shopping

M AMA AND DADDY are going off to the pipeline convention. Mama and my grandmothers finally decide I
am old enough to go with them on the shopping trip to buy
Mama a whole new wardrobe for the convention. I think a
shopping trip is just what Mama needs. She's been sad since
she lost the last baby. She just couldn't get over losing another
baby and had to go stay at that place that Daddy sends her.
Nobody is supposed to talk about it, and before she got home
from the mental hospital, Granny and Gramma packed up
all the baby things and Grampa took apart the baby crib, and
all that stuff got put away where Mama wouldn't have to look
at it. Instead, they made a reading nook. I had to look that

word up to see what it meant. I'm not sure you can make up for a lost baby with a new chair and some bookshelves under the window. Mama loves to read, but I never see her take a book there.

This house is not as big as ones we are used to. It's new, feels poky and dark, has a small yard and no trees, and is in something called a subdivision. You can practically see right into the neighbors' kitchen window from my bedroom. The boys are in one room with bunk beds, and Mama gets up ten times a night to make sure nobody's fallen out. When Daddy's real late or doesn't come home, she sleeps on the floor, like she thinks she could catch them if they fall. In my room, I still have the ballerina bedspreads, but the carpet is gray and the room small, even for twin beds. Granny and I share a closet, and now I smell like an old lady all the time. Sometimes I borrow Mama's perfume just so I don't smell like Granny.

I practically have to take a test before they let me go shopping with them. My whole life, I've watched as they get ready and drive off to this mystery. Afterward, I will be a grownup, and my friends will still be little girls. Things I have to remember:

- Never wear white shoes before Easter or after Labor Day.
- Never wear a straw hat or carry a straw bag before Easter or after Labor Day.
- If you are in the north, change Easter to Memorial Day.
- Never wear patent-leather shoes or carry a patent-leather bag. It's tacky, and people might see your underwear.
- Never wear trousers in public unless you are hunting or camping.
- Never hunt or camp if you can avoid it.

- Never wear shoes with ankle straps or open toes or platforms (my daddy calls them horeshoes, for some reason.)
- Never smoke, eat, or chew gum on the street.
- Never chew gum, period.
- Always carry mad money tied in a knot in your hand-kerchief. This is the same place you carry your collection money for church, but you have to tell them apart. I guess you need two hankies.
- Always be excited when somebody gives you another pearl for your add-a-pearl necklace. It will work out in the end. And, no, you'll probably never get enough for an opera-length necklace.
- A lady never wears diamonds before she is forty, and then only after dark.
- Never wear leather shoes with cocktail or eveningwear.
- Cross your legs only at the ankle, never at the knees.
- Never kiss a boy before you are engaged.
- Always be gracious and kind, especially to the less fortunate.
- Don't open Coke bottles with your teeth in front of any-body but family.

If you don't know all this stuff, or can't do everything on the list, you aren't ready to go shopping with the ladies in my family. Older ladies just know when you were ready, even when you don't know yourself.

Shopping is a whole new world of experience. It's reserved for special occasions only, like somebody getting ready to get married or go somewhere real special, like conventions. This convention lasts a whole week and always takes place far away, like Florida or the Bahamas or Cuba before the Revolution.

You can't wear just any old clothes to convention. Everything has to be new, except maybe some of your jewelry, if it is real old and important.

First, you take a trip to a neighborhood store for basics, to be sure that you will be dressed right for shopping. Your shoes and underwear must be able to pass the inspection of a downtown saleslady. You wear your best white gloves, so that when you take them off, your hands are clean and don't soil the merchandise. It means calling for an appointment and arranging for the car to pick us up.

On the day, I am so excited I can hardly stand it. Everyone is bustling around getting ready, and I am standing in a corner in my bedroom, trying not to get wrinkled or dirty. Henry David is playing with cars, and Samuel Taylor is playing with his feet. They are such boys and such babies, and not all grown up like me. Grown-up has some disadvantages—I think Granny may have stuck a hatpin right into my head, and my right shoe pinches my toes. The right one is my big foot. Everybody has one—the shoe salesman at Buster Brown told me so right after he X-rayed my feet. You just decide which foot you are going to fit. I chose wrong this time. He also told me that this was probably the last pair of shoes I would buy from him. I will have to go the ladies' shoe store from now on. Just another sign that I am all grown up.

I walk carefully down the hall to Mama and Daddy's room. Mama is sitting at her dressing table, sort of smoking a cigarette. I keep an eye on it, because sometimes she sets them down and forgets she's smoking, and a little fire starts. It's okay, because we have sand in decorative pots around the house, and we're pretty good at putting out little fires. Mama's decorative pots come from all over, and her collection got photographed for the parish newspaper. We didn't talk about what they are really for. But it's better if the fires never start, so I keep an eye on the cigarette.

The reading nook looks like the charity bin at church. Dresses are flung every which way, looking lost and unloved. Some of my favorites are there, discarded along with some obvious mistakes.

At the dressing table, Mama is staring into the mirror. I know from the watch pinned to the front of my outfit that the car will be here to pick us up in less than half an hour. She has that look about her, the one that lets me know she's going away in her head. She can't do that today. She can't do that to me.

"Hey, Mama. You about ready?"

After a moment, she responds, "Hey, yourself." She still stares in the mirror, and she's not really here. It is up to me to get her back from wherever it is she goes.

"Did I do okay? Do I look alright?" I ask, trying to reach her.

It feels like I have hold of one end of a long rope, and I am pulling her out of a deep hole. I can feel the change when she looks at me in mirror, and not off at something I can't see.

"Let me see." She blinks like she's just waking up, and swivels around to look at me. "You are getting so big. You're almost as tall as me."

I blush and beam as she examines me. I turn around so she can see me from every angle. She makes a little clicking sound, says "Come here," and grabs me by the bow on my dress. "Your grandmother can't tie a decent bow to save her soul, and don't you dare tell I told you so. Now, what should I wear?"

I help her pick out a dress, a suit, really, and gather the shoes and bag and hat that all go together. I fasten the pearls around her neck, and make sure the zipper isn't stuck so I won't have to cut her out of it later. We are ready to go just as the doorbell rings.

It is the car from the store, an old Rolls Royce with a driver's seat open to the air. It is silver and black, and has a half-naked lady standing on the hood. The driver, whose name is Roosevelt and who is almost as old as the car, wears a uniform with the shiniest buttons I've ever seen. I am torn between wanting to run down the front walk and jump into the car, and knowing that if I do, my shopping day will be over before it begins. I help Gramma up and help gather Granny's stuff and get them both started down the walk while Mama gives Annie Lee, the new help, last-minute instructions she doesn't need. I follow behind, wondering if I should use my wedding-march walk, which I got to use three times last summer when I was a flower girl or junior bridesmaid in a bunch of weddings for people Daddy works with who I don't hardly know. Those dresses went straight into the costume trunk. I decide to try it, but Mama takes my hand and squeezes it, saying "Uh-uh," but not like she's mad at me.

Roosevelt successfully wrangles the grandmothers into the car, and Mama follows effortlessly. He carefully arranges me in the jump seat and tips his hat and winks at me just before he closes the door. The big car pulls silently onto the road, and we sail away toward the adventure of the day.

Even Granny and Gramma are on their best behavior. They don't always get along, which Grampa says is because one of them is shanty and one is lace curtain, and they don't agree on which is which. It takes only a few minutes for us to pull up in front of J.P. Allen's, where we are greeted by name and ushered inside as if we were queens. Inside, Miss

Rose waits for us. She wears a plain black dress with an initial brooch, and her glasses with rhinestones at the corners are on a pearl necklace. I immediately start scheming about how to get me a pair like that, because if you have to wear glasses, and I do, they ought to look like that.

Mama introduces me. "Miss Rose, this is my daughter, DG. This is her very first shopping trip." Miss Rose fusses for a minute about how Mama couldn't possibly have a daughter as big as me, and compliments me on my pinching shoes, which makes them feel some better. She ushers all of us into a room lined with mirrors and fine old furniture. We sit, ankles crossed and backs straight, on a tufted sofa while a colored girl in a stiff white apron and gray dress serves tea and cakes from a gleaming silver service.

Mama pulls a piece of paper from her handbag. It is a list of "events" that she and Daddy must attend while on this trip, and she will need new clothes for all of them. Miss Rose's face lights up when she realizes just how much shopping is going to happen today. Mama has next to nothing to wear and hasn't been shopping for a long time. First, she was too fat, then she lost a bunch of weight, then she was having a baby, and then she wasn't. Then she was sad for a long time, so nothing fits, and besides, they haven't been on a trip like this for a couple of years, and Daddy thinks all-new clothes will make her happy again. Daddy thinks shopping will cure just about any ailment.

Miss Rose takes the list and disappears behind the mirrored wall. We sip tea and eat cookies. Mama lights a cigarette and I panic, because what if she starts a fire in here? I don't see any sand around, and figure this place would go up in a minute. I look around and try to figure out how to get out fast.

When Miss Rose returns, it is with a rack full of the most beautiful clothes I've ever seen. Loretta Young could sweep down the stairs in any of these dresses and dazzle the whole world. Mama and Miss Rose confer over the clothes, while my grandmothers offer their opinions on color and style and quantity. Once Mama makes her selections, a boy is dispatched down the street to Thompson-Boland-Lee for the suggested matching shoes and bag. Other salesladies assemble the jewelry, hats, gloves, stockings, lingerie, and other accessories that complete each outfit.

Mama disappears out of sight and reappears over and over, transformed into a sophisticated stranger each time. She is like some doll they dress up that doesn't have a choice in what she wears or what she does. Whenever she says yes to something, it is whisked out of sight, and something new and distracting is shoved in front of her. I think life with Daddy must be a lot like that. Something is always happening to take your mind off what is bothering you, unless what is happening *is* what is bothering you. She gets that faraway look again, and Gramma decides we're done for the day. It is time to head to the tearoom at Rich's or Davison's for sandwiches and maybe martinis, if it is late enough. I am already thinking that a Shirley Temple would be nice, and that maybe I could slip these shoes off under the table, and then we could go home, and I could put on regular clothes and just be me.

Another woman does the fitting, pinning here and marking there to let something out or down. Orders are placed for items not in stock and promised for delivery in time to be packed up in the new luggage that will follow Mama to St. Thomas.

The car glides away from the shops into the afternoon sunlight.

Chapter Fifteen

⊸ ⊸

1963 — Funeral

M Y GRAMPA DIED. In the bathtub. Of something called a cerebral hemorrhage. I had to ask somebody how to spell that.

Now we take him home to be with his people. To Illinois. Henry David was born there, and since he's younger than me, I guess I must have been there, but I don't remember it. All I know is it's a long way away up north, where every-thing is different. I asked Mama if we weren't his people, and shouldn't he be buried near us, but she said no, he needed to go home. To be with Bumpy and Mimi, who were his mother and father. Bumpy, Mama's grandpa, died before I was born, so I never knew him. There are pictures of me with Mimi when I was a baby, but I don't really remember her, except when I look at those pictures and close my eyes I can smell lavender and feel scratchy lace.

We have to fly to get there, and there's a big discussion about who should go and who should stay behind and where everybody will stay when we get there. Mama says we are all too young to go, and don't need to be involved with funerals, and everybody can stay home with Granny. I get to go, because I'm the oldest and Grampa and I were so close.

All my grownups act odd. Gramma sits and stares and doesn't answer questions. Mama doesn't cry. She is quiet and cold and gets everything done. Daddy is mad at everybody and everything. Being sad or scared makes Daddy mad, so he yells. They went to the funeral parlor to make arrangements for how we'd get Grampa to Illinois, and who would take care of him once we got there. Mama and Daddy were arguing about it when they got back. I guess it costs a lot of money to die.

Gramma is staying with us for now, because her house is too sad without Grampa. She shares my room, sleeping in the other twin bed while Granny sleeps with the boys. Gramma only cries when she thinks I am sleeping.

Gramma and Mama find no comfort in each other's company. I've always known they are angry with each other about something, but they never say what. Mama doesn't much like her brother, Uncle Teddy, who lives where Grampa will be buried. I didn't know you could not like your family until I saw Mama with hers. They are distant and unattached to each other. Mostly, our family is Daddy's family, but they have no part in this sadness. The only one of them who knew Grampa very well is Granny, and she's so used to people dying that it hardly makes her sad at all.

Uncle Teddy will be there when we get to Illinois. He plays the trumpet and has ten kids and a glass eye. Last summer, his whole family came to visit. They all drooped around because they're Yankees and not used to the heat. The boys got along just fine, but I could never figure out the girls. They are younger than me, and don't care about the same things I do, like drawing and books, mostly books. There's a couple of sets of twins in there, and they just wanted to talk to each other. Grampa told me just to call them all *cuz* and tell them it was a Southern thing.

Now I won't have Grampa to help me with stuff like that, and I wonder how I'll make out. Grampa was the best of all my grownups about explaining stuff and not making me feel too young or too dumb. I wish he was here to tell me what to do about funerals. As it is, I just wander around being quiet.

I've outgrown my Annette Funicello suitcase, and besides, it's too cheerful and silly to take to a funeral, so I go to the box room under the stairs to get the small suitcase from Mama's luggage. Not her train case, because she'll need that one, but the next-smallest suitcase that looks like marble and is all coral-colored silky material on the inside where it says Samsonite. Her monogram is on the outside, but that will be okay for just one trip. It should hold everything I need to take, though I'm not sure what I need take to a funeral. Grampa will (would) know, and he can (could) help me pick out the right stuff.

I don't have a black dress, and there's a discussion going on about whether or not I am old enough to wear one. Daddy doesn't think anybody should ever wear black, because Granny lived in black when he was a boy. Gramma thinks everybody in Illinois will be scandalized if we don't wear black. Mama is wearing her only black dress, but she says she never wants to see it again after the funeral. I pick out the two dresses that Grampa likes (liked) best on me. One changes colors when it moves, and the other is pink with ruffles. I don't much like the one with ruffles anymore, but Grampa always says (said) it made me look like a princess. I might like to be a princess, but I don't think that's ever going to happen. I'm not really the ruffle-y princess type, and I don't live near any princes. Mama sometimes sings a song: "I danced with a boy who danced with a girl who danced with the Prince of Wales." The Prince of Wales right now has big ears and is way too old for me.

The dress that changes colors is dark and mysterious, and sometimes it's blue, and sometimes red, and sometimes almost gray. I ask Mama how it works and she says "Magic," which I know isn't real, but feels like it could be when I wear this dress. Grampa doesn't (didn't) like this dress as much as the pink one, because he says (said) it makes me look older than I am. That's why I like it, and that's part of its magic. It gives a glimpse of what I'll look like someday—not old like Mama, but how I'll look when I'm about to be grown. I can almost see who I'll be then, and what I'll be like.

I'm not sure who I'll be without Grampa. Whenever I get mad or sad, he always makes me feel better. When I get in trouble with Mama and Daddy, he's never angry with me, and never makes me feel like he doesn't love me anymore. It's so hard to think of Grampa in the past, as gone as those other relatives I've never met. He doesn't feel gone, and I keep forgetting that he isn't coming back.

We will have to have two vigils. The one last night for his friends here, to say goodbye, and one when we get to Illinois, for all the people there. Gramma says it is okay to leave him where his mother is buried, since he was always a mama's boy. I like that he will have friends and family around, even if he doesn't have us. Grampa loved people and shouldn't be alone.

I don't go to the vigil. Daddy says there is no need to drag children to it. Daddy hates everything that has to do with death. From what I can make out, when Mama and Daddy came home, some of the pipeliners who were Grampa's friends had too much to drink and it got rowdy, more of a wake than a vigil. Mr. Fireball cried. Mr. Stumpy sang songs, and Mr. Dutch played the piano. Lots of people are sad about Grampa. It's funny to think of all of them dressed up and reciting the rosary, not in welding helmets and dirty overalls.

Everybody loved Grampa, and he kept all the men up and down the line equipped with anything they'd ever need. He could fix anything: machines, broken toys, bicycles, cars. He had the best spare parts inventory in the business. I don't know what happens now. My daddy is very handsome and knows everything about pipelining, but except for ironing and sewing, which he learned from Granny when he was a little boy, he can't do anything mechanical. Managing isn't something you can see or touch, it just happens. How will he find someone to replace Grampa? How will any of us replace Grampa?

Mama comes in to check my packing. She vetoes the pink dress because it isn't appropriate for a funeral. She chooses a navy blue dress that I am about to outgrow. She makes me try on the magic dress, looks at me for a long time with a funny look on her face, and decides that it is okay, too. I don't tell her that the shoes pinch because my feet won't stop growing. I can stand it for one day. She makes me leave off some petticoats so the dress will look sadder, more like a funeral than a party. She helps me pick out a chapel scarf.

Mama seems far away, and I'm worried about her. She doesn't cry about Grampa, and when I ask her why, she says, "Your Grampa and my father were not the same person." I've been trying to figure that one out.

The trip from Atlanta to Chicago is pretty long. We get up real early, and somebody from the funeral home picks us up in a hearse with Grampa in the back. It's a little crowded up front, and our luggage gets its own black car. Father Mike, who has traveled from Louisiana, rides with the luggage. He may be sadder than anybody but me and Gramma about Grandpa.

We get driven right out to the airplane on the tarmac. Father Mike says a prayer over the coffin before it's loaded onto the plane, then we all climb the stairs and find our seats. The stewardesses are real serious, since they know we are the bereaved. Daddy and Father Mike have whiskey on the plane while Mama stares out the window and Gramma sits stone-faced. I just read my book and think about how everything will be different without Grampa.

When we get to Chicago, it's the same thing all over again in reverse. They lower Grampa's coffin off the plane, put him in the hearse, and load Daddy and Father Mike up with the luggage because they've been drinking.

We go straight to the funeral home in a town called LaSalle to unload Grampa, and there is a big surprise. Grampa's sister Harriet is waiting for us! I didn't even know that Grampa had a sister! Mama breaks out in smiles and lets Great Aunt Harriet hug her neck for a long time. Gramma's face turns sour and she just says hello. I can't believe I have another relative that I didn't know anything about. How does that happen? I don't think it does in other people's families.

Even if somebody hadn't told me who she was, I would have known she was related to Grampa. She looks just like him, except wearing a dress and the highest heels on the tiniest feet I've ever seen! Kind of short; dark, almost-black hair with a white streak on the left temple sweeping back from a widow's peak; a round belly that even expensive clothes and corsets can't quite disguise. She looks at Father Mike and Daddy, who may have been drinking in the other car, sniffs, gets a nasty look on her face, and says, "What have you done with my baby brother?"

Daddy and the funeral director are explaining to Aunt Harriet all the arrangements that were already made down in Georgia before we got here, but she's having none of it. There is a couch in the private room they put us in, so I sit down, prop my book in my lap, and try to become invisible. You'd think Aunt Harriet was seven feet tall the way she stands up to Daddy, Gramma, and Father Mike. I think Daddy gets the most upset, because he got the best he could for Grampa, but it wasn't bonus time, and money was tight. Aunt Harriet says she will not have her brother buried on the cheap and buys new everything. She changes the service, even though Father Mike tells her that this is the way the church does it. "We'll do it my way, and if you don't want to do it, I'll find someone who will. There's a priest on every corner in this town," she says.

Gramma finally sits by me and doesn't argue anymore. Mama sits on her other side and looks sad. After a while, Daddy and Father Mike just give up and let Aunt Harriet have her way. When it is all over, she writes a check and smiles at everybody like they haven't just spent the last hour being hateful to each other.

Everybody starts gathering up their stuff. Aunt Harriet picks up a large handbag and carelessly grabs her mink coat from a chair. I've never seen a mink coat in person before. It looks so soft. I hope I get a chance to touch it. Aunt Harriet grabs my hand and throws the coat over one shoulder. Even though she is in high heels, I am almost as tall as she is.

"I want to get to know this girl," she says. "Brother told me lots of stories. I want to know if they are true. I have rooms at the hotel for everyone. She'll stay with me. The cars are ready outside."

Everybody does as they are told. Daddy looks worn out from arguing with her. Father Mike's hair, what little there is, is standing on end. Gramma looks like she wishes this all was over. Only Mama looks unfazed.

"Go," Mama says to me. "I'll see you at the hotel."

It's cold here. Colder than I'm used to, and when we get in the car, Aunt Harriet wrestles the coat off her shoulders and covers the both of us from the front. I'm wearing a mink coat. Sort of. With an unexpected relative. Who has closed her eyes and leaned her head back against the seat. Her face is small and white, with a gash of red lipstick that is beginning to smear. Up close, you can see where it bleeds into the tiny lines around her mouth. The coat is even softer than I thought it would be, and smells of Aunt Harriet's perfume.

"Why don't I know about you?" I ask.

Without opening her eyes, she replies, "Your father doesn't like me, and your mother isn't strong enough to stand up to him. What about you?" She talks to me like I'm a grownup.

"What about me?"

She raises one eyebrow at me, exactly the way Grampa used to. "Brother thought you were special. Are you?"

Well, I wasn't expecting that! Grownups usually ask you stuff like what grade are you in and do you like school. I think for a while, and the car glides on through the night.

"I'm pretty smart," I finally say. "And I like to read. A lot. So, I learn a lot of different stuff. Grampa and I used to do things together, like go to the junkyard and listen to ball games. And I can draw a little, like he did."

"He sent me a drawing you did for him. You are good for your age."

"Where do you live?" I ask. "Why have you never visited? Do you have kids I don't know about?"

"Let's see, we—my husband David and I—have an apartment in Chicago, but we live in Texas, on a ranch in a town called Weslaco."

Texas! I can't wait to get the map out and find Weslaco. It sounds exciting. "Do you have cows and horses? We lived on a farm for a while, but that didn't work out very well."

She laughs and says, "I heard your father tried cattle farming. I'm not surprised it didn't work. We have some cows, but mostly what we have is oil, lots and lots of oil."

The cars pull up to the hotel, and we are handed out by an attentive driver. Aunt Harriet flips the mink coat over her shoulder. The hotel manager rushes to meet her and helps to get everybody and their luggage off to their assigned rooms.

Aunt Harriet tells Mama again that I will spend the night with her, since Great Uncle David isn't here yet. Mama looks at Daddy, who you can tell wants her to say no, and then at me. "DG, what would you like to do?" he asks.

Daddy is looking right at me, but I keep looking at Mama, and ask her, "May I stay with Aunt Harriet, please?"

Daddy looks like I slapped him, but Mama nods yes, so I take my grownup suitcase and follow Aunt Harriet to the elevator. "It won't hurt anything. He'll get over it," she says as we walk away. I think this is the first time I haven't done what Daddy wanted.

When we get to her room, it turns out to be two rooms, almost like an apartment with a living room and bedroom. When I ask her why it doesn't have a kitchen, she laughs and answers, "Room service."

The furniture is very elegant, touched with gold, but not very comfortable, and the bedroom part has two enormous beds in it. I think I could learn to like traveling like this.

After we change into our nightclothes, Aunt Harriet offers to brush my hair. She carefully unbraids it and uses her very own silver brush to ease the tangles out. Then she takes down her own hair, which has been piled in an elaborate braid on her head. It falls below her waist, black with only threads of gray. As she brushes, she talks about Grampa.

"I was five when Neddie was born, and I loved him from the moment I saw him. Mam, that's your Mimi, wanted a baby for a very long time, but couldn't have one. He was unexpected. Showed up after she and Bumpy had given up. He almost didn't learn to walk, because between us, we never put him down to try. He wore dresses, all little boys did then, until he was two or three and got his first short pants. She kept his hair in long curls that she rolled up in paper wrappers every night. One day, Bumpy took him for a walk and brought him back without his curls. Mam cried for days, even though Bumpy brought the curls home in an envelope. She braided that hair and made bracelets for both of us. She knew that I loved Neddie as much as she did."

"Why do you call Mimi 'Mam'? Was that your special name for her?"

"She wasn't too happy when I showed up one day. Dollie, her sister and my real mother, didn't want me, just dropped me off and took the next train out of town. She'd have rather I called her Liza, but I was too small to say that. She didn't want me calling her Mama, so she taught me Mam. When Neddie came along, he was the one who called her Mimi. After Neddie, Mam didn't have much use for me. She couldn't wait to get rid of me and have Neddie to herself."

I've learned more about my family in five minutes with Aunt Harriet than in the whole rest of my life. I wish there was a way to write it down, but that will have to wait until I have time to myself. This story is better than books. It has abandoned children and wicked stepmothers and ranches in Texas and a mink coat.

In the morning, there is nothing to do but wait. We have room service breakfast. There will be another vigil at the funeral home tonight, but we are free all day. Gramma is spending the day with her brother and sister and Uncle Teddy's family. Daddy and Father Mike are still dealing with the changes in the funeral services. Aunt Harriet sends me off to bathe while she picks out what I'll wear today. When I'm done, I find her surveying my clothes in disappointment.

"This is all you brought?"

"Yes, ma'am. I have more clothes at home, lots more. But I didn't know what to bring."

"Wear this," she says, thrusting the plain old blue dress that I haven't quite outgrown at me.

"Yes, ma'am."

While I'm dressing, Aunt Harriet gets my mama back on the phone. I can hear her side of the conversation through the bedroom door.

"Is *HE* still there? Can you get away from him? Will you try? I thought we'd go into Chicago and do some shopping. Your daughter needs some clothes for this weather and I bet you do too. We'll be in the lobby in half an hour. We'll see you there." A pause. She listens and sighs in exasperation. "*I'll* talk to him if you can't. Just come."

She hangs up the phone and finds me sitting on the bed, ready to go. She brushes some imaginary lint off my dress and waves me into the sitting room.

"I'll be ready in twenty minutes. Don't answer the door or the phone." She sails off into the bathroom. I sit down to think.

I want to ask her questions, but I'm not sure what to ask. I sit primly on the couch in the sitting room, thinking of questions, crossing my ankles, and pretending that I am Audrey Hepburn in *Roman Holiday*.

Finally, Aunt Harriet bustles out of the bedroom dragging the mink coat. Today, her hair is tightly pulled back into a ballerina bun. She wears a silky dress, dark gray with tiny coral flowers, her slash of red lipstick, and pearls. She looks at me and asks, "No galoshes?"

"No, ma'am." I don't think we have galoshes in the South. I'm not quite sure what galoshes are, but I don't want her to know that.

"Well, let's hope you don't freeze to death dressed like that." That's a prospect that hadn't occurred to me. Grownups are always giving me something new to worry about.

We head off to the lobby. I worry Daddy might be there,

and I don't want to have to choose again. Mama is waiting, nervously. Aunt Harriet loads us into a waiting car, covers the three of us with her mink coat, and holds my mother's hand. I guess mink coats are always as big as you need them to be.

On the drive to Chicago, she tells stories about Mama as a little girl. "Every month, the boys who worked for my boss would drive me down from Chicago, and there would be your mother, waiting in front of the house, ready to go wherever I wanted to take her. I always brought a box of books with me, and sometimes paper dolls. We'd go downtown to the drugstore and have ice cream—no matter how cold it was, your mother always wanted ice cream."

"I only ever got ice cream when I was with you," Mama interrupts.

"If I didn't bring paper dolls, we'd pick some out in the drugstore or the dime store. Your mother loved those paper dolls. There were movie stars, like Shirley Temple, and famous women, like Amelia Earhart and Eleanor Roosevelt. And she took perfect care of them. They were cut out just so, and never bent or torn."

I think about the paper dolls Mama makes for me and swear to myself to take better care of them. I've never thought about it before, but books and paper dolls are something special that Mama and I share—mostly just the paper dolls, because she shares books with the boys, too. I think this is something that might be important to me when I am grown.

Mama and Aunt Harriet keep talking about people I don't know, like Great Uncle David, who is Aunt Harriet's husband and who isn't here yet. They talk about things that happened a long time ago and have nothing to do with me. I stay tucked in between them, mink hairs tickling my nose. I get drowsy, but when I hear something interesting, I let my head loll and my eyes close.

"You could come to me. It's not a bad little town, has good schools for the children. You could live in the guesthouse, there's plenty of room. There'd be horses and all kinds of animals for the boys. David's son is gone, and doesn't want anything to do with the ranch, just the money." Aunt Harriet's voice is soft and pleading.

"He'd never let me have my babies. There are too many things he can say against me. And what happens when I get… sick…again? You'd have all these children…."

"And plenty of help to take care of them. I have better lawyers than he can afford. We'll get your children." Aunt Harriet is pushing hard. I can feel her squeeze Mama's hand tighter in my lap.

"But I love him. What would I do without him?" Mama's voice is sad and resigned. I wish I could open my eyes, but I don't want to spook them. Aunt Harriet gives an exasperated sigh and drops Mama's hand in frustration. "You wouldn't get sick anymore if you left him. You'd be fine without him." Mama and Aunt Harriet stare out opposite windows of the car for the rest of the ride.

Shopping in Chicago is a lot like shopping in Atlanta. Everybody knows Aunt Harriet, and we sit in a private room and they bring her stuff. Mama and I try on what she tells us to, and she decides what to buy. Aunt Harriet reminds me a little of Flozella. They both act like queens or generals, and everybody falls in line.

Finally, she decides that Mama and I need better winter coats. Mama tries to explain that our coats are just fine for where we live, but Aunt Harriet is having none of it. A saleslady brings in the most beautiful coat I have seen. It is dark green wool and has a fur collar and a fur muff and a little fur-trimmed hat that ties under my chin, with fur pom-poms on the ends of the ties! A muff is something you put your hands in, so they don't get cold. I've read about muffs, but you don't see them much where we live. The inside of the muff is satin, and is the smoothest, coolest thing I've ever touched. I just might never take this coat off.

Then a salesman comes in carrying a mink coat. This one is darker than Aunt Harriet's. It almost matches my mama's hair. He slips it onto Mama's shoulders, and she doesn't look like somebody's mama anymore. She looks like a movie star. Mama laughs and twirls in front of the mirror, posing so we can admire her. Aunt Harriet tells them to wrap up every-thing but the coats and galoshes, which turn out to be rubber shoes that fit right over your regular shoes—that we'll wear those.

Mama stops posing and says, "I can't. You know I can't. *He* won't like it."

Aunt Harriet narrows her eyes. "Yes, you can. It's a present from me. It makes me happy to give it to you."

Mama gets a worried look on her face and says, "You know how he is. He won't...."

Aunt Harriet interrupts her. "We need to get back. We'll be late for the Rosary if we don't hurry."

Me and Mama follow her out, our new coats a little like a burden instead of a present. The car ride back to LaSalle is silent, but my hands are toasty warm inside my muff. The rest of the stuff we bought is waiting for us when get to the hotel.

Gramma, Daddy, and Father Mike are already at the funeral home, greeting people who came for the visitation and to sign the guestbook. The parlor and the chapel are full of people I don't know, along with all of Uncle Larry's kids. There are lots of particular things you do at funerals, and we are doing all of them. Ladies gather around Gramma and tell her how sorry they are. Gramma's brother and sister are here, but they seem dull compared to Aunt Harriet. I've met Great Aunt Martha and Great Uncle Kenneth before, but I don't really know them. They seem like strangers to Mama, too. Her side of the family is funny that way.

There's a little side room off the parlor, and when I wander by, I notice that some of the men are drinking in there. I drift back and forth between Gramma and Aunt Harriet, so I can listen to what's going on and keep an eye on the men wandering in and out of that room. It looks like all the men, even Uncle Teddy, Great Uncle Kenneth, Father Mike, and Daddy visit the room several times before we all go into the chapel and start praying.

None of this seems to have much to do with Grampa. Everyone prays for a long time, and finally, the priest releases us. Gramma looks exhausted. We all trail out to the cloakroom to start bundling up against the snow outside and the threatening wind. All the guests hurry out into the night, hoping to get home before the storm worsens.

Outside the cloakroom, Daddy's voice is loud and as cold as the night. "What is this?" He holds Mama's wrist tightly in one hand.

Mama's is softer and sounds more like a question. "A present from Aunt Harriet? She insisted?" The mink coat is on one arm but hangs where he has interrupted her putting it on.

Aunt Harriet enters the room and Daddy turns on her, twisting Mama's arm as he does. "You bitch." His voice is sharp like a knife, and he towers over tiny Aunt Harriet. "You keep away from my family. You hear me? You come near them, and you'll be sorry. The sorriest you've ever been."

He turns back to Mama and orders her, "Take it off." He drops her arm, and she stumbles forward. The mink coat slips from her arm onto the floor. He sees me and spits out, "Go get in the car, *my* car. You'll stay with us tonight." He is the scariest I've ever seen him. I do as he says, leaving my coat and muff behind. It is bitter cold outside.

When I reach the car, Father Mike is waiting, a little fuzzy from drinking. "What's wrong?" he asks when he sees the tears turned to sleet on my face. He bundles me into the car and finds a blanket to cover me with.

"Daddy's mad."

"Your father's just upset about your grandfather. He shows it by being angry. He doesn't like showing his soft side." I shake my head and tell him, "No. This is something else. This is more."

Father Mike is silent as my parents reach the car. My father barks out an order to the driver, and my mother shivers on the seat beside me. I pull part of my blanket over her, and she grasps my hand. We all sit silently during the ride to the hotel.

In the morning, I wake to the sound of my parents arguing. After a few minutes, an outer door slams, and my mama comes in from the bedroom. She wears a slip and some new bruises on her arms that won't show when she is dressed. "Good morning, Morning Glory!" She pretends to be happy, but her movements are jerky, and her voice is too cheerful, too urgent. "Time to get up and get dressed. DG, just wear the dress you had on yesterday. We'll fix your hair just before we go. Don't just sit there, DG, move."

My borrowed suitcase sits in a corner of the room, all my old things folded carefully inside. I get ready while Mama dresses and fixes her face. As she combs and braids my hair, I finally dare to ask, "What about our new clothes and stuff, Mama? Where are they?"

"Oh, DG. Don't think about that. Today is sad enough thinking about Grampa." There is the sound of tears in her voice, but she doesn't cry. "Aunt Harriet was wrong to inter-fere. She knows how your Daddy gets. He doesn't mean it. We'll all be home soon, and everything will be fine."

The rest of the day speeds by. I meet lots of people I'll never see again. I sit next to Gramma and she holds my hand the whole time, as if she thinks she might lose me the way we lost Grampa. Aunt Harriet sits next to a man who must be Uncle David a couple of pews behind us, and never speaks to any of us. Father Mike cries during the eulogy when he talks about Grampa.

It snows while they lower Grampa into the ground. When everyone else returns to the church for lunch in the base-ment, Daddy has us driven to the airport to catch an earlier plane home, leaving Gramma and Father Mike on their own to host the luncheon. He says we've been away from home long enough, that he misses his boys, and that he needs to get back to work.

We fly toward home and warm weather. I think about my lost coat and my sad mama, and this daddy I hardly know. But mostly, I think about Grampa, and wonder how I will make my way in the world without him.

CHAPTER SIXTEEN

⊹ ⊹

1964 — South Africa

DADDY IS MOVING US AGAIN, this time to South Africa. I don't mind going. Maybe Mama will be better there. Maybe Daddy will be different there. Maybe I'll be different there. Surely, *everything* will be different there.

We have all kinds of things to do to get ready to go. Passports and shots, lots of shots. Shots for things I've never even heard of—yellow fever, cholera, bilharzia, and more. Poor Henry David passes out every time he gets a shot, which makes Daddy awful mad. Daddy teases Henry David when it happens, and Henry David gets quiet and sad. The rest of us do okay, but now we all have sore arms. Samuel Taylor says his pitching arm is probably ruined, though it wasn't much to start with. Finn cries every time, and GeorgG, the baby, laughs and laughs no matter what they do to him. GeorgG's just happy to be included with the big kids for a change.

We land in South Africa in a place called Johannesburg, which sparkles all the time because there are so many gold mines. A fine coat of gold dust covers everything, even the poorest parts of town, making them beautiful in the sunlight. Even the dust on the furniture has gold in it. Mama says you could never get rich, even if you saved all the dust in your house for your whole life, but it might be fun to try. One week later, we are already on the move to Durban.

When we get to Durban, it looks a lot like Miami—palm trees, wide boulevards, and big fancy hotels along a beach called the Golden Mile. Everybody's excited about living near the beach. We all love the water, even the baby, Finn. It scares Mama to death to see us all splashing around in the Indian Ocean, even if we are only getting our feet wet. She can't stand to get her face wet, and Daddy jokes that she'd take an inner tube into the shower if he'd let her.

The road is lined with native rickshaw *wallahs* dressed in these elaborate beaded and embroidered costumes that look like something out of Mardi Gras, only they wear them every day. These men pull the rickshaws by long handles down the street at a run, then jump up between the handles and tip you so far back, you think you'll fall out. They compete all the time to see who can jump the highest and run the fastest, and who has the fanciest costume.

Wallah is an Indian word that means "in charge of," so you have rickshaw wallahs and shoeshine wallahs and tea wallahs and all different kinds of wallahs. They never call Daddy the pipeline wallah. They call him "Baas." The little kids along the line call him "Sweetie Baas," because he carries big bags of candy to hand out, and "sweeties" are what they call candy here. The people at the hotels along the beach have called him "Helicopter Baas" ever since he landed on the beach one evening, swirling sand everywhere.

Even when you are speaking English, it is a whole other language. Biscuits are cookies, and scones are kind of like biscuits, except with raisins in them. People here don't drink much coffee, but everybody drinks tea. Daddy is furious that his white workers have tea breaks written into their contract. They get to stop every day for "elevenses" at ten o'clock, which makes no sense at all. He'd never heard of such a thing on the pipeline! Pipeliners work daylight to dark, seven days a week, as long as the weather holds. Here, he works several crews, because people won't work more than forty hours, want to knock off at five o'clock, and won't work on Sundays. He says the natives are harder workers than the white folk.

One thing we haven't counted on is even though it's August, it's winter here, and the days are gray and sometimes rainy. It's really only warm enough to go into the water once in a while, and we don't stay long. These sirens start going off, and everybody scrambles for shore, so we do, too. When we get back to the hotel, we find out that those are shark sirens, not tornado alarms like back home. The boys want to go right back out to the beach, but I may not like the ocean here so much, after all.

My birthday is in three days, and I can hardly wait. I'll be thirteen. Mama says thirteen is a special age. She even has a poem she's going to read—a poem by Phyllis McGinley that starts off, "Thirteen is nothing...." Mama has a poem for everything. I've never worn a sweater on my birthday before. Usually, August is so hot, we can't hardly have a party at all. Of course, I don't have any friends here, so it won't be much of a party, and I'm feeling a little sorry for myself until my mama says I can go shopping and buy myself birthday presents and some souvenirs to take home, if we ever go home.

Things are sure different here, and it is hard to learn all the new rules, especially when they come at you in three different languages—and sometimes more. Mama says when we finally settle somewhere and start school, we will have to learn Afrikaans. Half the white people here speak English, and half speak Afrikaans, which comes from Dutch. Everybody has to learn both in school, but it ends up that they mostly just speak whatever they learned first. Daddy has to have a bunch of translators who can talk to people in about seven languages, though most of them are for the different tribes of Natives, which is what they call colored people here. Colored people are something else altogether. They originally came from Malaysia and married white people or Indians before it was illegal. The South Africans have uglier words for these people, too, just like we do at home, but we aren't allowed to use them. Mama would just kill us. She says words have the power to change people: the people they are used against, but mostly the people who use them. If you use ugly words, you become ugly.

Before we came here, I looked up South Africa in the encyclopedia and tried to learn everything I could. I read all the stuff Daddy's company sent home. Lots of it was really interesting, and some of it was strange. Mama says we must be on our best behavior all the time because we are representing our Daddy, our family, Daddy's company, and the whole United States. We might be the only Americans people ever meet, so we have to make a good impression whenever we go out. We must have on our company manners all the time and try not to make mistakes. Here, we must be real careful to only go in through white entrances, and not to talk to certain people.

When Daddy's not flying around in his helicopter, he has a driver named Clive. At first, I think it is crazy for my daddy to have a driver, since he's the best driver I know, but here they drive on the wrong side of the road, so maybe it isn't so crazy. Clive is teaching us all about living here. He says that in South Africa, there is something called *apartheid*, which is like segregation at home, but stricter. The natives, the Africans, outnumber the white people, so they have to be controlled. Most of them live in homelands, kind of like reservations for Indians at home—who are not the same as Indians here, who come from India and also have to live separately from whites and blacks. Then there are the Coloreds like Clive, who are part white and part something else, like Indian or native or Malaysian, and who have to live apart from everybody else. It is illegal for any of these different races to mix socially in any way. There are separate schools and separate housing, and the government tells you how much you can pay each kind of person. I know that we have segregation at home, but it never seemed so mean to me as it does here. They even divide the white people here into English and Afrikaaners, and they don't mix much, but that's because of history, not race.

All the people who aren't white work for white people in some way: housekeepers, yard boys, cooks, washerwomen. The white South Africans say it is their responsibility to give jobs to non-whites, so everybody has a lot of all-day, every-day servants. At the same time, I think they are afraid of them, because they so outnumber the whites. In the States, we used to have a cleaning lady, but not a different person for every job.

We have a nanny to help wrangle the boys now. Mama doesn't let her do much. And I have an *ayah*, which is like a nanny, but for older kids—and maybe just girls. Her name is Prateeka, which she says means *good example*, the perfect name for an ayah. Having her with me means I can go exploring without the rest of the family. Prateeka is very beautiful, small and dark with a single thick braid so long she could sit on if she wanted to. She dresses in *sarees* made of silk material that wraps around and around her until it makes a dress. The part in her hair is stained red to show she is married, and she wears a *bindi*, a red dot, in the middle of her forehead. Prateeka says she will help me pick out a saree and teach me how to wrap it. Prateeka is married to one of the Indian engineers who work for my daddy. She doesn't have any children yet, so he has given her permission to do this favor for my daddy, to help me understand this new country.

She looks very elegant in her bright colors and wears many gold bangles on her arms. I ask why she wears so much jewelry every day and she says it is her treasure from her wedding. People give a bride gold jewelry that belongs only to her and that her husband isn't allowed to touch. If she needs money for some reason that she can't tell her husband about like a present for him or money for her family, she can sell some of her bracelets and he will never know how much she has spent or loaned. Bad husbands might steal their wife's jewelry but then they are shamed by having a wife who wears no bracelets.

Prateeka has a good husband and her own university degree from the LPU in New Delhi where she lived before she came here to be married. LPU stands for Lovely Professional University which is where I want to go if I ever go to University. She studied to be an engineer like her husband but says it is better for a woman to be married instead of working. I never heard of a woman engineer so I guess she's right. She calls me Miss DG and makes it sound like tinkling bells.

Because it is my birthday in only three days, Prateeka and I are to spend the day shopping for whatever I want. Daddy has given me money and Mama too and I have money that I saved from babysitting before we came here. I am as rich as I have ever been and can spend it on anything I want.

First, we head to the spice market with Clive driving us. The open stall market stretches for miles. I have never seen groceries sold like this and didn't even know that there were this many different kinds of spices. Each shop specializes in only one or two. The spices are piled higher than my head. They have ordinary stuff like salt and pepper that we buy in bottles or boxes at home. Here, they measure everything out into tiny cloth bags or tin boxes that they seal up and then wrap like a present. Every shop we stop at makes a production out of selling me something. I must stop and have a seat and they must serve me tea like I'm a grownup lady who matters.

Everybody fusses over me at each of the shops. They love my red hair and freckles and even the fact that I am taller than most of them. Best of all, they like my accent. They think it's funny and laugh when I say words like after instead of *ahfter*. I tell them they have accents too, but that just makes them laugh more and wag their heads side to side. Whenever I buy something in one of the stalls, they always give me a small present as well. An older woman gives me a small jar of face cream that she says will make my freckles disappear. Prateeka speaks to all the shopkeepers in their own languages – Hindi and Tamil mostly. She speaks seven languages including

French, English, Afrikaans and Bantu, the most commonly spoken African language. Clive trails behind us, carrying our bags and boxes.

The spice market gradually turns into the Indian market where all the shops are owned by Indians. Prateeka tells me that India is a huge place, and her people speak many languages and observe many religions. She promises to take me to an underground Hindu temple to see some famous statues of a god named Ganesha, who has an elephant's head and makes all things possible.

We look at rugs and sarees and beautifully carved chests and tabletops, and my head spins. I have never seen so many beautiful things or smelled so many different smells. We choose a dark red saree for my mother, who will have to come back and be measured for the custom-made *choli*, the blouse that is worn with it. Both are embroidered with gold threads and will show off my mother's dark hair and pale skin to perfection. There is much discussion about what color I should wear, but the decision is very hard. I like one that is emerald green, but Prateeka and the auntie behind the counter think the color is too old for me. Finally, they choose a pale pink saree with soft silver paisleys.

I tell them that I am not allowed to wear pink because of my red hair—it clashes. They both insist, with the auntie telling me through Prateeka, that such people are mistaken. They wrap me up in the gorgeous silk fabric, and don't let me look until they are done. In the mirror, I see that I look completely different, like someone out of a book; graceful and willowy, not awkward and clumsy. The color is perfect against my hair and skin. Both glow in the dim light of the shop. They wrap up the saree and measure me for a choli that I will come back for tomorrow.

I am so excited on the drive home that I can barely sit still. I can't wait for Mama to see the things I've bought, and for the boys to play with the trucks I've bought them. Today, *I* am the Sweetie Baas, with candy and treats for everyone.

When we arrive back at the Princess Margaret Hotel, Clive drops us at the front and we carry our most important packages into the lobby, which is cool and studded with graceful white columns gleaming against elegant green walls. The room is dominated by a giant portrait of the hotel's namesake, Her Royal Highness Princess Margaret Rose. In the painting, she is dripping diamonds and pearls and looking sad. She came for a visit here after her family refused to let her marry the man she loved, because he was divorced. I read all about Princess Margaret Rose in a movie magazine when I was little. She stayed in the hotel, which was brand new then, and walked on the beach and cried for the man she loved. I made that last part up, but I can imagine her on the beach at night, alone and longing for someone she could never have.

As we make for the elevators, our arms full of packages, Mr. VerHoven, the manager and a stern Afrikaaner, appears at our side. "Excuse me, *jongfrou*," he says, addressing me and refusing to look at Prateeka. "You cannot bring your… this… *her* into the lobby of the hotel. It is not allowed," he stammers. His accent is thicker than usual.

I'm surprised, and don't know exactly what to do. Prateeka has lowered her head and begins backing away. I put my hand on her arm and tell him, "It's okay, Mr. VerHoven. She's with me. We're just going up to my rooms."

Mr. VerHoven is not satisfied. His voice is rising. He is angry. "Your *ousie*…" (he spits out the word, so I know it isn't nice) "…must go 'round the back, through the servants' entrance. She can't ride in the lift." He takes hold of her other arm as if to pull her away. I tighten my grip. Somehow, I am involved in a tug of war over a person in the lobby of a grand hotel.

Prateeka's voice is small, and doesn't sound like bells when she says, "Never mind, Miss DG. I will go to the back. I just forgot my place."

"But you're supposed to stay with me," I whine. I know the way she is being treated is terribly wrong. She is with me, my guest. I know I should do something. But Prateeka has slipped both our hands and is disappearing into some door I never noticed before.

"I'm not supposed to be alone," I tell Mr. VerHoven. "Now *I'll* be in trouble."

Mr. VerHoven relieves me of my packages, tells me that he'll explain to my mother, and directs me to the elevator. The uniformed attendant directs the elevator to my floor, and Mr. VerHoven marches me down the hall and knocks on the door. Henry David answers, takes one look at us, and announces loudly, "Mama, it's DG. She's in trouble."

Mr. VerHoven and I stand in the hall forever before my mother appears. She has GeorgG on her hip and her best company smile on her face. "Come in, Mr. VerHoven. Thank you for helping DG with her packages." She hands GeorgG off to the nanny and ushers us to chairs in the sitting room while tying a scarf over the curlers in her hair. "How can I help you?"

Mr. VerHoven looks uncomfortable. We have been nothing but trouble for him since we got here. Daddy insists that we all eat in the adult dining room at the regular time instead of the children's dining room at five. He lands a helicopter on the beach. We eat all the petit-fours at high tea. Mr. VerHoven thinks Americans are awful. He certainly thinks we are.

There is nothing hesitant about Mr. VerHoven, though, and despite his discomfort, he is very direct. "Your daughter has been breaking the law." Mama looks at me as if she believes this is not entirely impossible.

"Mama...." I start to interrupt but am silenced by my mother's abrupt "Hush!" and an upraised finger.

"What has she done, Mr. VerHoven?"

"She has brought her girl into the lobby of the hotel," he says, making "girl" sound as nasty as "ousie." "She was going to let her ride the elevator. I have made many concessions, madam, but this cannot stand. Many guests are offended. It is against the law. The law, madam!" Mr. VerHoven gets more indignant the longer he talks.

Mama's smile falters a little. She looks back and forth between Mr. VerHoven and me. "Mr. VerHoven, Mrs. Chandrasekhar was just looking after my daughter. That is all. If this caused a problem, I am sorry. She was doing what I asked her to."

Mr. VerHoven isn't finished with us yet. "You cannot just do what you want here. You must follow the rules. They keep us safe."

"I hardly think my daughter's ayah is a danger to anyone in this hotel, Mr. VerHoven." Mama's smile is getting thinner. She doesn't like arguing with people. It makes her very uncomfortable.

"Madam, you don't understand. She has taken your daughter to places she should not go. She knows the laws and her place and ignores both, using your daughter as an excuse and you as a shield. This cannot continue. You could be deported, or worse, detained. This hotel could be closed. I will have to ask you to leave if these activities continue."

I'm pretty sure the last thing we want is some kind of international incident. I'm sorry that something I have done has now spread to include my mother. I wonder if Prateeka will tell her husband, who will tell my daddy, who will be unhappy with everybody. We are just supposed to get along and go along. Everything runs smoothly and shouldn't attract daddy's attention except in a good way. We spend a lot of time making sure that nothing ever bothers my daddy.

My mother is speaking now. "I will let my husband know how unhappy you are, Mr. VerHoven." She stands, imperious in her scarf and curlers. "You may discuss the matter with him, if you think it necessary."

Mr. VerHoven has enough sense to know when to leave. He stands up, too, gives a curt little bow from the waist, and leaves, still in a huff.

Mama turns to me. "Oh, DG. What have you done? Now he'll tell your daddy and it will be a big mess, just like it was with you kids eating in the main dining room. These people don't like losing to your father. Go take your bath and get ready for dinner, then come help me with the boys."

Mr. VerHoven does not approach Daddy, that night or any other. Prateeka does not come again, and Mama sends away the nanny. We are followed everywhere by men in boxy suits who pretend that they are not watching everything we do. There is no party, and Mama doesn't read her poem. We leave Durban for Pietermaritzburg, at the foot of the Drakensburg Mountains, the day after my birthday and never return. South Africa changes us all.

Chapter Seventeen

ᕷ ᕷ

1966 — Runaway

THE PHONE IS RINGING as I come in the front door of our house in Atlanta. The phone is ringing, and I am positive that it is Bobby Lynch, who adores me past all reason. I grab it from the front hall table, yell "Got it," and, trailing the lengthy cord, barricade myself in the hall closet, where I am least likely to be heard. I breathe "Hello," in what I hope is an appropriately sexy voice.

It isn't him.

"Is your asthma all right?" comes the voice on the other end.

"Mama?" I ask, confused. She usually doesn't have phone privileges except on Sunday evenings, and, if I'm lucky, she runs out of time before she gets to me.

"I have to get out of here."

"Oh, Mama! I'll have Daddy call you when he gets ho—"

"NO!" She shouts down the line. "You listen. I'm not the crazy one."

Silence crackles on the line between us. I struggle to remember what I am supposed to say, and also that I am not supposed to cry.

"DG!" she hisses. "You have to listen to me. I am not crazy. The doctor says I am not the crazy one."

"Which doctor?" Maybe if I humor her a little, I can talk her off this latest ledge.

"The new one. The one with a beard."

I say his name, and she jumps on it. "That's right. Dr. Baronofsky. He says I don't have to stay here if I don't want to, because I'm not sick. There's nothing wrong with me."

"Oh, Mama, have you been taking your pills?"

"I don't need pills. I don't need to be here. I need to get out of here." She pauses, then says, "I need you to come get me."

For a second, I think I might throw up. I take a deep breath and tell her, "I can't come get you. I don't have a driver's license."

Off the hook, I relax a little. Soon, I can hand this latest mess off to Gramma or Granny or Daddy. But she comes right back at me. "You drive just fine. And don't say you don't, because I know you've taken that car out when you thought you could get away with it. You can certainly drive when I need you to."

Well, hell. I'm caught, and I don't even know how. That car will be mine when I turn sixteen but most of the time it just sits in the garage, except when my daddy is using it because his company car is in the shop, which it is a lot lately.

"Mama, I'd have to get on the freeway." So far, my clandestine excursions have been confined to meandering back roads.

"There's nothing to it. Just don't drive too slow. Oh, and wear something that makes you look older, so you don't get pulled over."

A vision of Audrey Hepburn in *Breakfast at Tiffany's* slides through my head as I wonder where I'll get a long cigarette holder.

"Mama, I don't think I can do this. I don't think you're supposed to come home yet. You still need to rest."

"I don't need to rest. I don't need to stay in this place a minute longer. I need to come home."

"Daddy can talk to your doctor," I respond reasonably.

"The doctor has already spoken to your father. I don't want him involved in this. What I do now, I am doing without him. I'll have the doctor call you back in a few minutes. You stay by the phone. He'll call you right back."

Then she's gone, and I am holding a light blue Princess phone that matches the flocked wallpaper in the front hall, hoping that one of my grownups comes home before the phone rings again.

When it does, it's Daddy, saying he won't be staying at home tonight, just stopping by to drop off the boys and pick up his overnight bag, which I should pack and leave in the front hall. He doesn't have any time to talk, and I don't find a way to tell him about Mama. I know where he will be when he should be with us, handling this mess.

I don't tell Bobby any of this when he calls. Our conversation is punctuated with long pauses while we contemplate the profundity of life. He knows my mother is away, everybody does, but he doesn't know where, or that this has been going on for most of my life. He doesn't ask me questions about her; we have more important things to talk about, like his painting and the big project he's creating in his mother's garage for his year-end open-option exam, and how awful the war in Vietnam is.

The phone rings again, and the doctor, who seems to think I am my mother's sister, says yes, she can come home, but must be picked up by a responsible person, which I am pretty sure is not her license-less fifteen-year-old daughter.

The phone rings again, and my mother gives me detailed instructions. Be sure to wear something appropriate. Wear more makeup than I usually do, but not too much. Don't wear that horrible frosted pink lipstick, wear something darker; it will make me look older. Just this once, I may borrow her good pearls. Have the car washed. Again, don't drive too slowly on the freeway, but don't drive too fast, either. Be sure the tank is full of gas before I leave home. Mr. Phelps will fill it up on credit if I tell him Daddy sent me, but there should be money in her everyday handbag. There's a tear in the lining, and she hides her mad money there.

"You can do this," she says. "I know you can."

"But Mama, shouldn't Daddy come get you? He's responsible for you…."

"You heard the doctor. You heard him say I could come home. You heard him say I'm not crazy."

We don't use that word when we talk about Mama. Mama is tired, needs to rest, is not feeling like herself, is away for a while. But never crazy.

"But Mama, Daddy…."

She cuts me off so sharply that I am not sure I've heard her right. "I am not the crazy one. *He* is. Come get me tomorrow."

She is gone, and I am left sitting at the back of the hall closet surrounded by tennis rackets and baseball bats and winter boots and apprehension. My world has turned upside down, and maybe I'll just stay in the closet forever.

But I don't. My parents have brought me up to do as I am told, and who will tell me not to do this thing? I could tell Granny, who can't drive and who would make me tell my father, who would almost surely be very angry, which is something we always try to avoid. I could tell my gramma, but she hates my daddy, and they always end up arguing, and she doesn't drive, so she's no help, either. I can't tell anyone else, because we don't talk about where my mama goes when she's gone. I can't even tell Bobby Lynch, who has a driver's license already, because I'm not supposed to let anyone else drive that car, and because it would change the way he thinks about me.

I spend that evening scrounging through my closet for something appropriate to wear for breaking my mother out of the mental institution where she has lived for the past three months. I finally settle on my new funeral dress, which is dark gray, more appropriate for my age than black, and which is so long it comes almost to my knees.

When the house is quiet, and everyone has gone to bed, I slip into my parents' empty room and into Mama's closet, a place that has always been a refuge for me.

The faint scent of Shocking by Schiaparelli fills the air. As the bottles of perfume reach the end of their usefulness, Mama removes the lids and the sprayers and stashes them about the closet, so everything she wears carries that scent lightly. I trail my hands over fabric and boxes and think about what she has asked me to do. I can't reach my father on the phone, because he hasn't told me where he's staying.

I could try the two-way radio in the garage, but he must be in the company car to hear it. I help myself to Mama's best pearls, to the car keys and mad money from her everyday purse, and, on a whim, to her alligator pumps and matching handbag. I search the drawers to find a pair of dove gray gloves that are softer than baby skin. Finally, completing my raid, I climb the footstool, grab a hatbox, and escape to my own room. I spend the rest of the night trying to create a hairstyle that will accommodate both my waist-length hair and the Jackie Kennedy pillbox I've appropriated for this escapade.

In the morning, I realize I have forgotten darker lipstick, but with trying to convince Granny that I am sick enough to stay home from school, but not sick enough for her to have to skip bridge, I decide I will have to go with chewing on my lips to make them darker.

I can drive pretty well, but the idea of the freeway fills me with fear. I slow to a crawl as I approach the on-ramp and then pass it, speed up, and drive around the block to make another pass at it. I have carefully planned my route so I need not make any left turns.

On my third try, I hold my breath, straighten my arms, lock my elbows, punch the accelerator with Mama's alligator high heel, and hit the highway. There is a map on the front seat, carefully folded to display the route I will follow. I wonder how people keep track of all the signs they have to read to navigate a road like this while keeping their speed up and wrangling a mess of kids in the back seat. I don't even have the radio on now, and I'm distracted by everything that rolls by. The other traffic ignores me, even though I am driving slowly. It takes all my concentration just to stay in my own lane.

By the time I am halfway there, I stop flinching at every car that passes me, and I am driving a daring fifty-five miles an hour (the speed limit is seventy) and hoping I don't miss the exit sign. After an hour or so, I glide down the exit ramp and into the quiet town of Milledgeville. I negotiate the town square, and after only two passes, make the correct turn onto the road where the hospital is.

It isn't a scary place like the state hospitals found on the other side of town. It is never a state hospital, but always a place whose exterior belies the sadness inside. This one is a lovely antebellum mansion at the end of a sweeping drive lined by ancient oak trees—Tara revisited. The places always seem to reflect the cultural myths of the local area. The guests, as they are called, sit in white rockers on the wrap-around galleries, their feet tapping in unison. Colored help slips unobtrusively among them, passing out lemonade and the drug of the hour. Nobody is chained to the beds here, at least not where visitors might see them. The horrible things happen out of sight. I only know some of them, the ones my mama thinks are not too terrible to tell me.

I pull up in front, and wish I was driving a more imposing car than a Camaro painted British Racing Green. I open the door, swing both legs out of the car, and stand up. I wobble a little in my unaccustomed high heels, and hope people will think it is because of the uneven caliche-covered drive and not my innate clumsiness. My stomach is somersaulting something awful. I am fifteen, usually look twelve, and am hoping to be taken for twenty-five. Up the steps and inside, I do not remove my oversized sunglasses as I sign the visitor register with my Aunt Elisabeth's name. I am sure that if I am caught, Mama and I will be sharing a room here. I am directed to her room by an orderly who doesn't look much older than me. Nobody stops me or calls my bluff. Slightly more comfortable in my high heels, I swing my hips a little and wonder if that boy is watching.

When I open the door to her room, Mama is sitting on the edge of the bed with her train case clutched on her lap. She is wearing a green plaid shirt, pedal pushers, and Keds on her feet. She does not look crazy, though someone has given her a bad haircut.

She visibly relaxes as I close the door behind me, and says, "I thought you'd never get here." I think I might cry. "Take this." She thrusts the train case at me. "Did you park the car out front?" I nod, and she says, "Fine, that's fine. You take that," indicating the luggage, "out the front, and then bring the car around back, where they drop off the deliveries. That's where patients check out." She doesn't meet my eyes, and I know she is lying to me.

"Mama...." I really am going to throw up. I've done something awful and I will surely go to hell for it, but not before both my grandmothers and my father are done with me, and I'll never get a driver's license, and won't get to go to Junior Prom with Bobby Lynch, who has said he'll go even if he doesn't believe in proms, and that car will sit in the garage until the wheels drop off before I'm ever allowed to drive it again.

Mama has me by the shoulders and gives me a gentle shake. I am taller than she is in high heels. "DG. Stop it. Stop thinking. Breathe. Go get the car. I'll meet you in the back."

I make it back to the car, wondering where all the attendants are and why somebody doesn't stop me, but thankful that rest homes are easier to break out of than institutions. I imagine that the state police will be called, and that we will be arrested on the way home. At least I am driving legally, since my learner's permit requires a licensed driver to accompany me at all times. It doesn't state that the driver must be sane, though that probably goes without saying. By the time I swing around back, I am breaking out in hives, and any minute will probably need my inhaler from the silk belly of my mother's alligator handbag.

Mama is peering out the screen door, waiting on me. She waves at someone out of sight and skips down the steps. She looks like the teenager I am supposed to be. She swings open the passenger door, hops in, laughing, and sings out, "Let's go, DG, let's go. Get me out of here now!" She is happier than I have ever seen her.

"Heavens, child! You'll ruin those shoes if you drive in them."

CHAPTER EIGHTEEN

✧ ✧

1966 — Revelation

IT'S BEEN SIX MONTHS since Mama ran away from the hospital, and, in a lot of ways, she's been running away from her old self ever since. She's changed her hair and the way she dresses, and she even has a job, sort of. She's an Avon Lady, and now knows more about makeup than I do. She throws parties and does makeovers, and she's a new woman most of the time.

She still has bad days sometimes, but not as often, and she gets better pretty fast. The biggest difference is that she never used to let us know when she was upset. Now, she's mad at Daddy all the time, and it shows in the ways she talks about and to him. No more waiting for supper till he gets home. No more ironing his shirts herself; she sends them out to the laundry for extra starch, so they scratch his neck. Still, some days she doesn't get out of bed, and I get worried that it is happening again, the darkness that pulls her away from us, but it passes now in just hours, not days or weeks. She is truly with us now, and not staring off into the distance.

Daddy sure was surprised when he came home after a couple of days and found Mama home and Granny packing to leave. He surely didn't expect to find her checked out of the hospital. I think he tried to persuade her to go back, but she was having none of it. Mama asked him right out where he'd been and what was he doing. He kind of stuttered out, "Working." Mama snorted and replied, "That's what you always say. Do you think I'm stupid?"

After that, they went into their bedroom and continued arguing. We never used to hear them fight. I was always pretty sure they did, from the way they acted after, all stiff and uncomfortable with each other. Now, we hear them yelling at each other whenever Daddy comes home. Daddy doesn't like her working, since sometimes it takes her away in the evenings. I kind of like it, because I get to babysit, and I get paid fifty cents an hour, so I can make like five dollars a week, plus my regular allowance. I save up to buy record albums, or maybe even a new record player one day, so I won't have to share one with the boys.

Sometimes, when they fight, Daddy gets real mad and leaves. He's not used to people disagreeing with him or not doing what he tells them to. He expects everybody to kowtow to him all the time. Lately, we've been reading the newspapers before he does, and we just eat the last banana without worrying if he might want it. Mama encourages these small rebellions. The boys go off to day camps, and I go charm school at one of the big department stores. They teach us all kinds of things, and at the end, we get to be in a fashion show in the tearoom. Everybody's mothers and friends will come to watch us parade around in our Bobby Brooks or Villager outfits, which are included in the cost of the class, and which we get to take home at the end of the show. Some of us may even be chosen as Junior Department models. Mama says I don't have to wear my headgear while I'm at charm school if I promise to wear it every minute that I am home. The headgear, with its straps and wires, looks like a catcher's mask, and I absolutely hate it. I even get to ride the city bus downtown with my friend Mona.

Even charm school doesn't make up for how strange things are between Mama and Daddy, and how Daddy is also acting weird with us kids. They are both too polite with each other, and with us. Daddy looks at Mama like she's grown a second head, and he doesn't know what she'll do next. Daddy brings home special treats for us every day, like Matchbox cars for the boys and books or magazines for me, like *Glamour* and *Seventeen*. Mama told me to watch out, that he was just trying to buy us off, but it's nice that he thinks about us for a change.

I can't decide which is worse, the arguments or the times they don't talk to each other at all. Everything is strange all the time. Granny has gone to stay with Aunt Odilia, and it is nice to have a room to myself for a change, but still, I'm nervous all the time. I feel like I do just before a storm blows in: the air is heavy, and the color of the sky is not quite right. If I'm not careful, I might just get blown away. Even the boys notice something's wrong and are on their best behavior.

The storm finally breaks one evening after the little boys are in bed. I've just brushed my teeth, and I'm carrying a glass of water from the bathroom across the hall to my bedroom. I get to stay up pretty late, since it's summer and we don't have school, but the boys have a regular bedtime. At one end of the hall is my parents' bedroom, and other leads into the kitchen and family room. Their door is open, which is a good sign, since they always close it when they argue. I pause to call goodnight.

They are both sitting on the end of the bed. Mama has been crying, and Daddy looks grim and tight-lipped. He waves me into their room, saying, "Come here. We need to talk to you."

The hall telescopes away from me, becoming impossibly long. It takes forever for me to reach their doorway. I lean against the doorjamb, one foot in their room and one in the hall, poised to run away. Daddy's face is hard and mean. Mama's legs are jiggling a mile a minute. For a moment, no one speaks, then Daddy says, "Your mother wants a divorce. I can't change her mind." Tears fill my eyes and I blink them away, trying to really see these strangers for the first time.

"Your mother and the boys will stay here. I'll get a place of my own. I want you to come with me. Live with me." I feel like something has sucked all the air out of the room. I struggle to breathe while he continues, "You, you are all that matters. I don't care about the others, but I want you with me." My mother sits silently beside him but flinches at his words as if he has slapped her.

I cannot look at him any longer without crying, but I will not give him that satisfaction, so I turn my head toward the hallway and see Henry David at the other end, standing there, his beautiful face shattered. The hallway telescopes in and out again and I know that he has heard every word. I draw a ragged breath and try to hold my voice steady. "No. I won't go with you. Not anywhere. Not ever."

It is his turn to look stunned. He is saying things to me, but I don't hear them. All I can hear is blood rushing in my head. I look back down the hall to Henry David, but he is gone. I hear the sound of a door closing, a door that won't open again for me.

I turn and walk to my room, careful not to slam the door. I sit on the end of my bed and wonder what our lives will be like without Daddy. Even though he's gone a lot as it is, Mama has always made sure that he is a presence in our lives. Now, even the idea of him makes me feel sick, as if I've done something wrong. Why me? Why did he do this to me?

In the morning, my father is gone, and my mother is reading the want ads, looking for a real job. "It will be fine," she tells me. "He'll have to pay child support. I just need a job, so we can have the extras. It will be an adventure! Think what we'll learn about ourselves."

Three months later, it doesn't seem like much of an adventure. My mother, who hasn't had a job in twenty years, still can't find a good one. Any skills she once had are out of date. She and the boys spend the days hanging notices on door handles or dropping telephone books on front steps for about what I make babysitting. The boys don't get paid, of course. She takes them with her so I can babysit for money while she's gone. It is hot and exhausting work, and they come home wiped out. I now babysit as much as I can, saving for school clothes instead of a record player. I charge a dollar an hour, because of my extensive experience as a big sister. People are comfortable leaving even their tiniest babies with me. Nobody dies in my care, though GeorgG, my own brother, does fall and break his two front teeth on the curb when I step inside to make a phone call.

My father calls every day, but Henry David and I refuse to speak to him. We don't speak to each other, either. There is a wall between us that neither can breach. My mother lets the other boys talk to him and then takes the phone, long cord trailing behind her, into the bedroom for a more private conversation.

One evening, she calls me to her room. She is too thin and darkly tanned from working outside so much. "He's coming back. I've decided to take him back," she tells me.

I am so angry I can hardly speak. My stutter makes my words almost unintelligible. "Y-y-you c-c-ann't. D-d-d-don't do this," I sputter. I am shaking so hard I think I might shatter.

My mother reaches out and tries to hold me, but I break away, and she settles for my hand. "DG, I can't do this alone. I thought I could, but I can't. This is no way for us to live. I do think he's changed. He really misses us. He wants his family back." Her voice begs me to understand.

"He doesn't change. We do. Did you forget what he said to me?"

My mother looks at me blankly. "He didn't mean all those things. Surely you know that. We were just angry and trying to hurt each other. It will be different. You'll see."

My father returns like a conquering hero. The little boys, who don't understand anything, are delighted have him home. He brings bicycles for them. The older boys get dirt bikes. My mother gets a mink coat, a match for the one Aunt Harriet bought her years ago that he made her return. "DG," he says. "What do you want? Your mama says you're too young for a fur coat. Tell me your heart's desire. I have no hard feelings." His eyes are warm, his smile open and welcoming. He is a spider spinning a web. He terrifies me now.

"N-nothing," I tell him, struggling not to stutter. "I want nothing from you."

He is quiet for a moment as his eyes harden and his smile tightens. "Oh, but you will, DG. I can wait. You will."

CHAPTER NINETEEN

❧ ❧

*1967 — Tea
at the St. Francis*

I STUDIOUSLY IGNORE THE RINGING TELEPHONE, even though it seriously interferes with nursing my broken heart over Bobby Lynch, whom I've had to leave behind while Daddy drags us halfway around the world again, this time to Australia. But the phone doesn't stop, which in my family means a disaster, so I put my broken heart on hold and answer: "What's wrong?" which is an improvement over my Granny, who answers, "Who died?"

Sam T's changing voice croaks, "Hank says you have to come."

"Oh, no I don't. It's y'all's turn."

"You have to. Mama's bringing the Hare Krishnas to tea."

Crap. Crap. Crap.

I'm off the bed, scrambling into shoes, running for the elevator in about five seconds flat. If I can distract her, we can take them somewhere besides the dark-paneled lobby of the St. Francis. It's the hotel where Daddy's company puts up everybody as they transit through San Francisco, and it is real important here that we look like the perfect family.

In the lobby, Sam is standing by the house phone, clutching a Gump's department store bag and looking like the end of the world.

"Where's Hank?" (Henry David has decided he wants to be called Hank after some book he read. Daddy now calls him "Cow Dog.")

"He sent me to tell you. Then he went away."

That's what people are good at in this family, going away. Going away is my family's best thing.

I can already hear the ruckus—tambourines jingling, bare feet slapping marble, voices mumbling at a low roar—as Mama swans past the top-hatted doormen who bow politely, then stiffen as they realize what's coming. Mama is trailing her new mink coat, along with a bedraggled clutch of strangely subdued young people wearing saffron-colored robes and nearly bald heads sporting oddly-angled pony tails.

I start for the door, but am intercepted by Mr. Merriwether, whose calm surface is belied by the white lines around his tight mouth and the panic in his eyes. Things like this do not happen in his hotel. Mr. Merriwether wears a morning suit every day and does not panic.

"But, Madam…."

Mama interrupts him imperiously. "We'll be twenty-five or so for tea, Merriwether. In the dining room, I think. The parlor is far too small. Extra sandwiches, please." Mama is channeling Queen Victoria from an old Irene Dunne movie, and will brook no discussion.

She tosses him the mink with the contempt it deserves and leads her cavalcade to the pristine dining room while Sam, Mr. Merriwether, and I bring up the rear. He looks at me as if to ask if I might intervene and stop this madness, and I tell him, "Not a chance. Not when she's like this."

He is clearly flustered and blowing fur out of his face. "But, Miss, this is most irregular. Those…people…."

"Those people are Mama's guests."

Mr. Merriwether scowls, hands the mink to me, and follows Mama into the dining room. Now she is a general deploying her troops to her best advantage. Mr. Merriwether cannot displace them without a scene, and Mr. Merriwether's principal job is to avoid scenes at all costs.

Mama circulates among her guests, placing a napkin on a lap here and gently shifting an elbow off a table there. I find her handbag in a chair and drop off the mink on top of it in a heap of disrespect, as if it were the centerpiece in a game of hot potato.

Mama beckons me to another table and introduces me to the peculiar guests encircling her.

"This is my daughter, DG. She studies art. DG, this young lady is Sunflower. She's a musician. Doesn't she have the loveliest eyes you ever seen?"

Sunflower clutches a tambourine to her chest, is visibly dirty, smells like she hasn't bathed in weeks, and has eyes like Elizabeth Taylor. Mama presses my shoulders lightly and I find myself seated at a table with the strangest strangers I have ever encountered.

Like the well-bred Southern lady that I am, I finish the introductions and begin the small talk that will propel us through the rest of the afternoon.

"Where are you from? How do you find San Francisco? Have you been here long? Do you enjoy your work? Have you visited Chinatown yet? Is Haight-Ashbury as a magical place as it sounds in all the music?"

I get mostly monosyllables in reply as I try to track Mama around the room. She pats Mr. Merriwether soothingly on the arm and sends him to the kitchen. In moments, an army of starch-shirted, tuxedoed waiters descends bearing all the trappings of high tea—with extra sandwiches. Small talk is replaced by the silence of eating.

Our guests are around my age, none of them very much older. They are wary of me and this place, and they, too, keep an eye on Mama as she flits about the room, Lady Bountiful dispensing smiles and touches and extra sandwiches. Sam and Hank drift into the room and are pressed into hosting duties at other tables.

Sunflower and the others stare at the quantities of dainty food heaped before them. I press sugary petit fours and crustless sandwiches on them. After a few minutes, their self-consciousness fades and they begin to eat in earnest, as if they have not had their fill for a long time. They are polite and quiet and still a little afraid, as if they think they will be run out of here at any moment.

Mr. Merriwether and his staff conduct themselves impeccably, as if this is not the scruffiest group to whom they have ever served tea. They only occasionally wrinkle their noses at a smell or a particularly dirty neck. Mama summons Mr. Merriwether and whispers something in his ear. He nods and disappears again.

When everyone has eaten all they can, Mama begins making her goodbyes. She knows most of their names, and their wary faces light up as she talks to them. She begins to gently herd them toward the doors that will deliver them out into the streets again. I know sometime later today, they will be bused back to a compound, where they will clean and chant late into the night. I think I am not cut out to be a hippie, after all.

Mr. Merriwether materializes at the door with a large picnic basket and a sigh of relief. He passes it to Mama, who smiles like the sun at him. She hands the basket off to a tall boy called Ram with bad teeth and a pouch full of flyers and books. He looks stunned as she leans in, kisses his cheeks, tells him (not too loudly) "Call your mother," and sends him and the others off to meet their futures.

Mr. Merriwether still hovers, and Mama reassures him that everything will be taken care of, that he was ever so helpful, and that she assumes all responsibility, financial and otherwise, for the afternoon. Later on, she will pay him from her pin money.

We drift into the elevator, exhausted from being on our best behavior and worrying about what might happen next. Sam still clutches the Gump's bag, and Hank is dragging the bedraggled mink behind him. As the doors close, so do Mama's eyes, and her shoulders sag.

"Don't tell your father. I looked at them and saw you... you and the boys. I couldn't stand that they were hungry." I guess that Mr. Merriwether is just lucky that she couldn't stand that they were dirty. "Shake that thing out, Henry David. It looks like something the cat dragged in."

The doors slide open, and we progress toward our suite of rooms. Inside, a hotel-provided nanny supervises the younger boys, and tries to keep the baby from teething on the wooden furniture and shoes.

CHAPTER TWENTY

❧ ❧

1967 — Honolulu Airport

T HE HONOLULU AIRPORT is as crowded a place as I have ever been. Sunburned vacationers, soldiers toting heavy duffle bags, and costumed greeters in grass skirts and flowered loincloths all vie for attention in the brutal humidity.

We are our usual assemblage of luggage and anxiety. Today we have more of both, since we are traveling with Daddy, and that puts everyone just a little on edge. Mostly, we are a well-oiled traveling machine, with each of us in charge of assigned bags, both carry-on and checked, and our appropriate traveling documents. The suitcases are numbered, and everybody keeps track of their stuff. It just works.

But not when Daddy travels with us. He often travels alone these days and doesn't remember what it takes to get all of us on the road. Plus, he's used to being in charge, and doesn't like it when we get on just fine without him. He's trying to resurrect his reputation within the family, and probably for a wider audience, so we are all always together now. The perfect picture of the perfect family on parade.

My brothers are all wearing ties and crewcuts, while Mama and I wear stockings and heels and dresses, since Daddy believes that ladies don't wear pants in public. It doesn't matter that our flight will be sixteen hours long.

I have removed myself, my bag, and my book to a seat several rows away from the traveling circus that is my family. The chairs around me fill up with soldiers: boys, really, who are only a couple of years older than me. They want to talk about things like surfing, cars, and where we're all from and where I'm going. They don't want to talk about the things that haunt our television set every night at dinnertime, or where they are going. The conversation lags, and I look up to find Sam, who seems worried.

"Daddy wants you. Now." Poor Sam has a deep, serious voice that is misplaced in such a small boy. His shirttail is already a little untucked, and I think that by the time we reach Australia, he will be an embarrassment.

"I'll be there in a minute," I tell him, and make my good-byes to my assembled admirers. Some of them press addresses scribbled on bits of paper into my hands and ask for postcards or pictures that I will never send. As I walk away, one of them calls, "Don't forget me." I think I never will.

I watch my family warily as I approach them. Since Mama and Daddy got back together, I don't think I'll ever feel at home again. The boys struggle to incorporate

Daddy's instructions into the routines they have already memorized. It isn't going well. Mama is walking around, bouncing the fussy baby on her hip. The younger boys are lining up the carry-on luggage and trying to sort it by bearer. There is a flurry of activity—then, everyone freezes, and Daddy has Hank by the arm. Even from here, I can tell he is angry, and would like to shake Hank. He won't, of course. Not in public. He won't even raise his voice, but Hank will feel his anger. Abruptly, Daddy sticks a hand in his pocket, pulls out a money clip, hands Hank some cash, pushes him, and says, "...and don't come back without it." Hank trudges away, and I can tell he dreads whatever he has been told to do. I am torn between catching Hank and finding out what is going on.

Mama turns back just in time to catch this pantomime, and as I reach them, she hands off the baby. Even he is quiet now, as if he senses imminent disaster.

"Where's Hank going?" Mama asks.

Daddy glares at her and says, "He left my briefcase at the hotel. I sent him back to get it." Mama's face crumples in dismay.

"Oh, Al. How could you?" My father just sent a twelve-year-old boy off to make his way across an unfamiliar city to a hotel we've already checked out of to find a missing briefcase. Even by my father's standards, this is outrageous.

"He was supposed to keep track of it." There were things Hank was supposed to keep track of, but Daddy's briefcase was not one of them.

"I'll see if I can catch him," I tell Mama, handing the baby back to her. My father's hand on my arm stops me.

"You aren't going anywhere. You've been whoring around this airport enough...."

I jerk away from him. Usually, frustration or anger silence me, as my stutter overwhelms any attempts at speech—but not this time. Months, maybe years, of accumulated rage pour over the carefully constructed dam of ladylike demeanor I live behind.

"Fuck you! I'm not the whore in this family."

My mother chokes out, "DG. Don't. Stop, now."

But it is too late. My father reaches for me again, and I plant both hands on his chest and push. He is so shocked that he stumbles backwards, and lands sprawled in a chair with his mouth hanging open.

I loom over him. "You don't get to talk to me like that. You don't get to treat me like that. You don't get to treat any of us like that." I shake and I spit, but I do not yell, and I do not stutter.

"We are not a bunch of dancing bears you get to trot out to impress people. We have lives when you're not even here. We...."

Mama takes my arm and pulls me away. "Stop it. Go to the ladies' room and wash your face. Now." Still shaking, I storm off. By the time I reach the ladies', I am running out of steam and can barely stand. What have I done? What will he do? I am too worked up to cry, and too scared to go back. What am I going to do? I stare at the girl in the mirror, and wonder who she is. I slump against the wall.

Women come and go, and some ask me if I need help. "No, ma'am. Thank you," is my polite reply. I mill in and out of different stalls, trying not to attract attention.

A kind woman with lots of Kleenex and too much makeup tells me, "Honey, you're going to have to go back out there. Whatever it is, it can't be so bad." I'm afraid it is so bad that I can't even imagine what will happen next.

Outside the door, Sam waits for me. As we walk back toward the rest of the family, he takes my hand and squeezes it.

Mama and the rest of the boys sit with our assorted carry-ons. The baby contentedly chews on a luggage tag. I sink into the chair beside Mama and wait. I have no idea what to say.

"He's gone after Hank. He just called me from the hotel. They are on their way back now. Hank is fine."

"Oh, Mama. I'm sorry I made such a fuss. I'm sorry I swore."

"Hush. When he gets back, don't say anything. Don't give him an excuse to notice you. Keep away from him, and he'll ignore you. Just keep your head down. You and I will talk about this another time."

They return, and it goes as Mama says. We bustle off to board amid the usual comments and compliments on the size of us and how smoothly we operate. I make myself as invisible as a tall, skinny redhead can be.

Halfway to Australia, Sam croaks, "You don't stutter anymore, do you?"

I think about it for a minute, and tell him, "No, I don't."

Chapter Twenty-One

✎ ✎

1968 — *Dinner at Antoine's*

IT'S BEEN ALMOST TWO YEARS since I spent any time with my father. Our disagreements and my anger have become too great and I keep my distance. I know he's angry with me, too. The difference is that it's scary when he's angry with you. It's like you stop existing. He doesn't care, doesn't even understand if you are angry with him.

The best way to describe him is like a lighthouse beacon. As long as you are in the warmth of his regard, it seems the best place to be. Safe and bright and beautiful. Outside of his regard, there might be monsters—cold, dark, scary. Of course, even when he's angry with you, *especially* when he's angry with you, you aren't really outside of his regard. You're never truly safe.

Out of the blue, using Mama as an intermediary, he asks me to join him for dinner. Not a family dinner—just the two of us. "Go," she says. "He's trying be nice. It'll be a chance for the two of you to make peace. He's been so careful lately. Please."

My stomach knots. I wish I could disappear. I wish I was strong enough to really defy him. I wish I could say no. I wish I could run away. But it is important to Mama that there is calm in the family. I cannot leave her and the boys alone with him. I console myself, knowing there's a job coming up that will take him to a place we cannot follow, and we will all be free of him for a while. I have a plan to leave shortly after he does. That way, they'll have time to get used to me being gone before he gets back. They'll be moving again to another new home and won't notice me missing from a place I've never been.

Reluctantly, I say yes.

Mama makes all the arrangements, since I manage to avoid Daddy most of the time. She is excited. "It will be just like old times. You'll enjoy yourselves. You'll both get over this unpleasantness between you."

She doesn't know that she voices my deepest fears. That I will get over it. That I will develop a sort of amnesia, convince myself it's not so bad. That I will be ensnared again.

On the Saturday of our dinner meeting, I am waiting in the downstairs hallway as the clock strikes seven. It pays to be ready before he is. He makes his entrance from the master bedroom, impeccably turned out, looking more fifty than seventy, still handsome with a smile that can take your breath away. Bespoke suit, handmade shoes, tailored shirt. Distinguished. The kind of man you want to be seen with.

One who increases your value in the world when you appear in his company.

He eyes me head to toe. I pass inspection easily. I got a whole new outfit out of this, whatever *this* is. My mama's shopping talent at its best. The dress wouldn't have been my first choice, but it does make me look very sophisticated. A deep, rich purple that complements my skin tone. Mama has done her best taming my auburn hair, and it hangs long and perfectly straight for once—though, of course, as soon as I step out into the New Orleans humidity, that'll be over. She's even done my makeup. Since her stint as an Avon Lady, Mama's become a fanatic about not going out without her face. Today, she's leveled that fanaticism at me. I must admit that the results are pretty nice. I don't look like I'm wearing makeup at all. I just look like a better version of me.

Daddy opens the front door and escorts me to his car. Like his clothes, his manners are impeccable. His car is long and low and obscenely fast. Across the bridge from Mandeville lies New Orleans. The car slips into the French Quarter and deposits us at the restaurant after only a few minutes of strained conversation. An obsequious valet hands me out of the car while fawning over my father and his toy.

The maître d' greets us by name; we've been eating at Antoine's as far back as I can remember. I had my first Shirley Temple here. I suspect Antoine's keeps files on everyone who eats there. When we live near enough, we have all our family celebrations here. I wonder what Daddy is celebrating tonight.

We are escorted to one of the side booths, with a red leather banquette and red velvet curtains can be pulled to discreetly shield diners from prying eyes. This evening, the curtains are open, and we watch the comings and goings of the restaurant while Daddy eats his Oysters Rockefeller. Daddy orders a whiskey for himself and a Shirley Temple for me.

"I am always sorry you can't enjoy shellfish," he says, pointing out a deficiency that has irritated him my whole life.

"You don't miss what you've never had," I reply pleasantly. I will not take his bait. He thinks my allergies are all in my head. I am terrified of accidentally eating something that might kill me. My father finds this funny.

"Snuffy Smith may join us," he says, switching the topic. "I'm taking him on the Nigeria job. Let's play a little joke on him."

I haven't seen Mr. Snuffy since I was little. Daddy likes practical jokes, and though he hasn't laid out what this one involves, I agree to go along, because, well, what else can I do?

"Call me Al, and just go along with whatever I say. Ask him about his name when I introduce you." I am confused, because I don't know where he's going with this. I am uncomfortable, but no more so than I've been all evening. Daddy's being extra charming, which always unsettles me, and the staff is falling all over themselves to cater to his every whim. I always want to scream when nobody can see through him to what he really is. I'm off guard and out of practice in dealing with him.

When Mr. Snuffy arrives, the situation grows more awkward. He obviously doesn't recognize me. Daddy doesn't introduce me. He just sits a little closer and drapes his arm across the booth behind me. I want to squirm in discomfort, but deportment classes have ensured that I don't. I still don't understand what the joke is. As instructed, I express surprise at Snuffy's nickname, and feign genuine interest as I ask him how he got it. I know what's coming. He tells a long, complicated story that doesn't make any sense, or answer the question of origin. All pipeliners with nicknames do this. Even my daddy. I have never understood a single one of them.

I sit between them, trying to figure out what is happening. They discuss the upcoming job in Africa, and the hazards and rewards of working in a war zone. I wish Hank were here when they start talking about equipment and pipe size and how many feet they can lay in a day. He loves that stuff.

I remember to smile and nod and look interested, which I am, a little. I am always interested in what goes on in the world, now that I have traveled in it. The war is in Nigeria, a civil war between most of the rest of the country and a place called Biafra. I have seen pictures in magazines and on TV about the terrible aftermath of this war. Mama and the boys and I can't go with Daddy, because the company is uncomfortable with families living anywhere in Africa right now. They can't guarantee our safety, not even on a company compound, and so won't pay for us to come. The men who go will live offshore on barges and work from there as much as possible, and they will get hardship bonuses and generous holiday and travel allowances. They'll also get extra life and accident insurance in case anything goes wrong.

Several drinks in, the bragging starts. I nurse my Shirley Temple. Daddy slips me money to go to the powder room and winks at me. I still don't understand what the joke is.

When I return to the table, Daddy is gone and I have a new drink waiting—not a Shirley Temple, but a real cocktail, something sweet and sticky that tries to hide the taste of the alcohol. I slide into the booth, leaving room for Daddy to sit on the end when he gets back. Mr. Snuffy sits there, a little bleary from drink. I've been told to call him Clark, which is apparently his real name. I remain in character. I'm still not positive what that character is, though I imagine I am supposed to be a slightly mysterious young woman nursing her drink.

Still sipping my drink, I try all the conversational tacks I can think of, and brightly ask a series of questions: "Did you enjoy your supper? How long have you known Al? Is he a good boss? Do you enjoy traveling so much for your job? Won't it be scary to go to a place where there has been such a terrible war, and that doesn't sound very safe? Do you live near here? Where are you staying?"

His replies are mostly monosyllabic, but at the last one, he names a hotel in the Quarter near here, and pulls a key from his jacket pocket. "Let's go," he says, and takes my wrist and pulls me up and out of the booth before I can object. I feel shaky and a little dizzy, like I stood up too fast, and my stomach swirls.

"Where's Pete?" I ask. I try to look like I'm not being dragged across the restaurant, like the nice girl I am, not making a scene, not scared to death.

"He'll show up later. At the hotel. Just because it's me instead of him shouldn't make a difference."

I finally understand the joke. I'm still not sure who Daddy's playing it on.

Shaking and near tears, I assess my situation. I could cry out for help, but the street is full of drunks, and every other place we pass is a dive bar or a strip joint. The crowd doesn't care what happens to me. I have no money for a payphone. I have no ID other than my driver's license, in my purse with my inhaler. No way to get home. Nowhere to go. My desperation grows, and I decide that at Mr. Snuffy's hotel, I will get away, even if I have to make a scene.

I make my play at the elevators just off the slightly seedy hotel lobby. "Stop! I'm not who or what you think I am. I'm his daughter. This is supposed to be a joke. You have to let me go. Please, let me go." I'm still keeping my voice down, but I am dug in. This is my last stand. I'm not going any further, no matter what happens. I start jerking my arm away from his rough grasp.

Mr. Snuffy turns his glassy eyes to mine and tries to understand what I've just told him. From behind us comes a voice, sly and nasty in tone.

"Well, well. What do we have here? Just what are you doing with my daughter, Snuffy?"

Mr. Snuffy drops my arm and stares open-mouthed. He's a whole lot soberer than he was a minute ago.

"Nothing...I thought...I was...." he tries to stammer his way through an explanation for a situation he doesn't really understand.

Then the laughter starts. Daddy claps Mr. Snuffy on the shoulder, saying, "I got you. I got you good."

Mr. Snuffy narrows his eyes and laughs, too. He looks at me like he's not sure about all this.

"Tell him. Tell him, DG."

"That's right, Mr. Snuffy. You've known me since I was a little girl. You used to have that dog, the one who did tricks. He told me it was a just a joke. I'm sorry. I'm so sorry."

Mr. Snuffy is still looking back and forth between us, confused. I hope I will never have to see him again.

Daddy tells me to have a seat in the lobby while he takes Mr. Snuffy up to his room. I sit down, cross my ankles, fold my hands over my clutch in my lap, and wonder if I look like a whore.

Daddy reappears later, much later. He stands in front of me and says, "Let's go." A valet appears in front of the hotel with the car, and we drive home in silence. He stops once on the way, so I can throw up the cocktail he ordered for me. Mama is sitting on the couch in the living room waiting for us. She is eager for news.

"Was it nice? Did you have a good time?"

Daddy tells her that Snuffy Smith joined us for dinner, and that they talked a bunch of business. He tells her that I had a real cocktail. I tell her that dinner was nice, that the Quarter was crowded, and excuse myself to bed. Daddy has made his point.

CHAPTER TWENTY-TWO

⮌ ⮌

1969 — *Strangers on a Train*

T HE TRAIN SWAYS, lulling everyone else in the compart-
ment to sleep. Across the aisle, my brothers are piled up
like puppies. My mother sits watchdog-like, her legs stretched
across the door to prevent unauthorized entry.

I compose myself into a picture of perfect melancholy.
Forehead pressed against the window glass. My slightly damp
eyes are a little unfocused in a middle-distance stare. My
glasses are in my lap. I can't actually see anything, and my
eyes water from the struggle to focus. A slight Mona Lisa-like
expression plays about my lips (I hope). I cheat a look at my
reflection. Almost there.

I am practicing this tableau for later use in cafés or on park benches, so I can intrigue the local boys. But I really am sad! Really!

We've been riding the rails in Europe for almost six months. Mama reminds me that it is not, in fact, riding the rails unless you are hopping on and off boxcars while being chased by railroad bulls, so I guess what we are doing is cramming ourselves into tiny train compartments, stopping sometimes in little towns to stay in small family hostels in which the W.C. is down the hall and the showers are communal.

Mama came up with this plan after Australia. For my father, Australia was a nuisance with difficult labor laws. For the boys, it was a world of sport with football (soccer), rugby (football, almost), cricket (baseball without bases), tennis, swimming, you name it. Australians are sport mad! For Mama, it was a lot of work. As usual, she made us live away from the company housing and other ex-pat compounds; in neighborhoods where "real" people live and attend schools that "real" children attend.

"Why travel all the way to the other side of the world if you're just going to pretend that you're in America? I've met Americans all my life. Let's meet some Australians!" she said, part of her new attitude toward life, which is that everything is an adventure and that we always enjoy ourselves.

Which is in direct conflict with my great two-fold sorrow. I am determined to enjoy nothing and, that as often as I can arrange it, nobody else will either. Especially Daddy!

We left home for Australia just after my junior year which was the pinnacle of my entire life! I was in love with Bobby Lynch in Atlanta, who loved me back. Our life as artists stretched out before us, perfect in every way. My teacher entered some of my work in a regional competition for young artists and I won. First Place. A full scholarship to the Savannah Art Institute. And best of all, early admission! They were going to let me start immediately! That meant I didn't have to go to Australia, that I could stay where I wanted to for once.

But Daddy greeted this prospect with less than enthusiasm. "We're only just back together as a family," he protested. "We couldn't stand to be without you."

He pretended to consider it for a while. "Perhaps there's a way we can work it out." "Maybe you could live with your Grandmother."

But finally denying me this chance, "You are too young to be left alone while we're half a world away. You'd never manage on your own." "Your mother needs you. You can't just desert your family."

And ultimately, "No. You are going with us. No more discussion."

Not that there'd been any discussion to begin with. My father is an absolute ruler. Nobody challenges his authority. I begged, pleaded, threatened, promised, and did everything I could think of to get him to change his mind, but never stood a chance against his quiet certainty that I belonged with him.

Australia turned out to be a lot like America. Big wide-open country with lots of big, wide-open people. Friendly. Eager to point out similarities, frontiers and gold-rushes and Viet Nam. The drinking age was sixteen. I took some advantage of that and discovered that I'm not an alcoholic like my Grampa or a lightweight like my father who's over his limit after one shot or two beers, but a hollow-legger like my mother.

When she found out I wasn't just dancing in bars, my mother sat me down and explained her strategy. "Drink something with ice in it, Jack and Coke or gin and tonic, and ask for extra ice. You can get a lot of mileage out of one drink. The ice melts and you never need a refill. Don't try to out-drink somebody just because you think you can. Avoid fancy cocktails. All that stuff mixed together isn't worth it. Always ask for a glass if you're drinking beer. Ladies don't drink out of beer bottles. Never order at the bar. It doesn't look nice. Don't let your father find out that you are drinking."

This advice kept me mostly out of a trouble while I spent my senior year cramming for national exams that would gain everyone else entry to one national university or another depending on your scores and me nothing.

Then my father jumped ship, changed companies, began planning for a new job in a war-torn Nigeria that had no place for us. My mother took us all back to Mandeville for a while, looked around and decided she wasn't going to sit and wait on my father with a Christmas tree still standing decorated in April and our lives on hold until he decided to notice us again.

That's how we end up on a train somewhere is the middle of Europe with our luggage piled under our feet and the pugs, Scott and Zelda Fitzgerald snoring louder than all four brothers.

The pile of boys and dogs comes alive squirming, the former complaining about elbows and feet and casting accusations of farting. I sigh deeply. My life is desperate enough without this noisy crowd that is just so embarrassingly American.

My mother marshals her troops. First, we figure out which country we'll be disembarking in. Hank is in charge of travel language so he checks train schedules and maps and calculates the difference between kilometers and miles. Sam alerts us to the kind of food likely to be available at our next port of call. Finn manages lodging and advises us where we'll be staying and what kind of bathrooms to expect. GeorgG, only six, sorts the luggage and gets the dogs onto leashes and into their carriers.

My mother, at some point and with a bit of whimsy, decides that each of us will specialize in a particular aspect of the foreign languages we'll encounter. No one of us can read, write, or speak an entire foreign language. Since she pretends that our travel is educational, we spend much of our time in museums, studying art and history. Because of my previous interest in art, my mother decides that I should be the one to focus on what I now call Museum European Languages. Yes, I can read and translate museum placards in French, Italian, and German. Occasionally, I get a break and some out of the way museum will have anticipated English-speaking tourists. But not in France. Which is where I think we might be now. France is a good place to use my melancholy look.

Mother manages travel documents and money. Our first stop is always the American Express Office, where we convert money to the local currency, verify that our pensione is safe and livable, and check for cables from my father. Her solution to figuring out money in different countries is to hand the clerk, waiter, or shop girl a wad of currency and let them sort it out.

Even when he's not with us, Daddy tries to control everything we do. From a distance, we get to ignore much of his overbearing influence. Once a week, Mother has us write him letters, at least one page about what we've been doing and where we are. We indulge in polite fictions, like "We miss you." or "I am looking forward to hearing about the last river crossing. Are you still sacrificing pigs to the river gods?" or "Scott and Zelda peed on the rug in the pensione this week. Fortunately, it is not an antique."

We continue this haphazard wandering for most of a year, crisscrossing western Europe on rattling trains, stopping for a while when something in Fodor's catches my mother's eye, moving on when she grows bored.

CHAPTER TWENTY-THREE

꙳ ꙳

1970 — *Runaway Redux*

WE'VE BEEN BACK IN THE STATES for three months now. I'd say home, but that's not quite right. We are never home. This time, it's Texas, just outside of Houston. My father's plans remain unclear. He interviews first with one company, then with another, and never seems to settle. None of them has a job that appeals to him. He is gone days at a time—looking for work, or so he says.

The boys enroll in local schools, but me, I'm in limbo. A matriculation certificate from a high school in Australia means nothing in Texas. I stubbornly refuse my mother's efforts to get me into high school here. "I'm done with that," I tell her. "You can't make me."

Most days, I don't get out of bed. There's no reason to. I have no place to go. I know no one in this new subdivision, miles to the north of Houston. The nearest grocery store is almost an hour away. I am trapped and can't figure out how to escape. I can hardly remember how to breathe.

My mother comes to my bedroom door, to see if I need anything and to find out if I'm getting up. I grunt answers, and she goes away. Some days, she insists, and I get up, shower and dress, and follow her around while she runs errands: grocery shopping, dry cleaning. She tempts me with the promise of a shopping expedition, new clothes, new anything to get me to emerge from my cave.

Daddy threatens to send me away to a hospital if I don't straighten up. I hear them arguing. Mama is adamant; she says no, and so far, he won't cross her in this. I don't speak to him. I am a silent indictment of the crime he has committed against me. It burns inside me, and I can't let it go. I had a full scholarship. I was going to the Savannah Art Institute. I was going to have a life that didn't include him. He stopped it. I was too young, seventeen, to leave while the family went to the other end of the world. I couldn't be left alone like that. It wouldn't be safe. It wouldn't be right. I begged and begged but had to watch as my scholarship went to someone else. I watched two years of my life, first in Australia and then in Europe, happen to someone else while I hid deep inside. And now, this move to Houston.

Then, one day, she doesn't even knock. She sails into my room, rips open the blackout curtains, and lays three items at the foot of the bed.

"Enough," she says. "Get up. You are letting him win. I have a plan." She is as excited as I've ever seen her. I struggle to roll over and sit up.

All I can offer is a sullen, "What?"

My mother does have a plan. It involves a GED study guide, a candy striper's uniform, and a college course catalog for a downtown junior college, the items currently adorning the foot of my bed. She tosses the book to me. "You are a really good test-taker, always have been. You're going to take this test, and…"

I interrupt her. "What are you talking about? I can't take a test and get out of here."

"Yes, yes, you can," she tells me. "This is your way out! Listen!"

She spins out her plan, and I slowly begin to believe her. "You study for this test. It will get you the same thing as a high school diploma." I start to protest, but she hushes me. "I'll get you a tutor if you need one. Once you have a diploma, you're going to enroll in college…."

I interrupt her. "He'll never let me. Where will the money come from? How am I supposed to do this?"

She grins. "I have it all figured out. I can get the money. But you, *you* have to get out of bed. *You* have to start caring."

She thrusts the pink-and-white uniform at me. "Try this on. If it doesn't fit, we'll get another one." I slip out of bed, intrigued, and shuck my nightgown. "You are signed up as a bookmobile volunteer every Thursday. You are going to go downtown, to St. Joseph's Hospital, and spend the day handing out books and reading to people. You can do that, can't you?"

I nod. It doesn't sound like much of a plan, but I'm listening. My mother takes a deep breath and continues. "On Monday, Wednesday, and Friday, you put this uniform on, and drive downtown to the South Texas Junior College and take classes. You can change into regular clothes in the bathroom once you get there. I know it's not Savannah. I know it's not what you dreamed about. But you *are* getting out of here. Even if it kills us both. *You* are getting out."

Still dressed like a candy striper, I fall back on the bed. "Where will the money come from? College costs money, and we don't have any. Just what he gives us, and it will never be enough." Maintaining my bleak mood in the face of my mother's excitement is a challenge, but I muddle on.

"I figured it out. I can save enough from the grocery money to pay for it. We'll just eat Hamburger Helper when your father's not home. Not as much Coke and chips. The boys won't know the difference."

I stare at the ceiling of my room, and wonder who this woman with a plan is. She's different, focused and determined, and she's aiming all that determination at me. My mother tosses me the course catalog and keeps her momentum going. "Look, they have courses in art and history and literature and everything. You could take a rodeo course, if you wanted."

"But what happens when he finds out? He'll kill us both." I know he won't kill us, not really—but we'll wish he had.

"We are going to surprise him with your grades. Your good grades. Your excellent grades. It will be something he can brag about: his smart daughter in college, getting excellent grades. This will work. I know it will. It has to." My mother is running out of steam and is looking at me, pleadingly, begging me to care about something again.

"What do I have to do?" I ask her. This slight response sets her off again.

"The next semester starts in just three weeks. So you've got to study and take this test, and pass it before then. I bet you can pass it today. I've got the application for the college in my purse. We'll fill it out and take it in. Then you register for the classes you want. Maybe you don't take a full load the first semester, maybe just three classes. That way, we don't need as much money right away. I can save up more for later, and you can take as many classes as they'll let you. We'll figure out when to tell him, how to surprise him when the time is right. You *can* do this. I know you can."

My mother's confidence is contagious. What if this works? What if I get out of here? I reach for the GED study guide like it's a lifeline, and slowly pull it toward me. I am afraid to hope, to believe—but at the same time, I very much want to.

The next few days pass in a blur. I spend my first Thursday at the hospital, handing out books. The other days I spend at the Junior College library with a math tutor who wears thick glasses, and whose heavy Chinese accent keeps him mired in junior college when he should be at a real university. We exchange skills. My near-perfect diction for his love of numbers. I am more successful at improving his English than he is at improving my math.

I take the GED exam and the SAT on the same day. When I present my scores along with my application, there is a kerfuffle over the difference in my verbal and math scores. My mother explains that they can investigate my long history of standardized test scores showing the same thing. I'm very good at subjects that require language skills, and very bad at those that require math. I am enrolled on a probationary basis.

Our deception lasts a little over six months. My brothers do not starve. My uniform spends most of its time wadded up in the back seat of Hank's car, which he lets me use while he takes the bus or mother's car to school. I take English

101 and American History and a drama class, but avoid art classes. I learn that the War of Colonial Rebellion was, in fact, the American Revolution, and practice spelling harbor and labor instead of harbour and labour. I meet people and go to cocktail parties at faculty members' houses, and to bars on Montrose with boys who admire the way I dress, and on dates with boys who press me for sex in cars.

All along, I pretend I am taking extra volunteer shifts at the hospital, reading to the ill and dying. My father brags about my dedication to my volunteer work, but worries that I meet only sick people and nuns, never doctors. I make up amusing anecdotes about people I see only once. He believes I'm spending four days a week at the hospital. I take early classes, and do my homework in the library before I make the long drive home each day.

My mother spins her own lies and collects brochures for finishing schools abroad, in England, Switzerland, and France. She tells him that I'll attract a better quality of husband if I am properly turned out, and one of these places will be perfect for the task. "Just think of the young men she'll meet when she visits stately homes!" she tells him. My father reminds her of the cost and the distance, and the unlikelihood that anyone would ever want to marry me.

I ask for and receive permission from my father to take a part-time job at the downtown Foley's store. I become a floater. They tell me on Thursday evenings where I will work on Friday and Saturday, which store and what department. I can work any cash register, and can sell anything from junior clothing to lawnmowers. Sometimes, I am pulled to run the old-fashioned switchboard because I have a "classy" accent. I am a quick study. I save enough to get my own car, a used Mercury Cougar that overheats when you run the air conditioning. I make a sort of life from these things.

A counselor at the junior college helps me complete an application to the University of Texas at Austin, and sends my transcripts in. One day, when I come home, my mother is waiting for me with an envelope, fat and full of the future. My hands shake as I open it and look at the unfamiliar documents: an acceptance letter, an application for housing, and another one for grants and loans to offset costs.

My mother and I sit in our rarely-used living room and wonder how we will tell my father so he thinks this was all his idea, and wasn't he so very clever about it all? How will we get him to say yes? Flattery goes a long way with a man like my father.

My mother launches her direct offensive one night at dinner, the table set with china and silver. She has bundled the boys off to the movies, and it is just the three of us and his favorite dishes. The fat envelope sits by her plate, looming larger and larger the longer it goes unmentioned. She is animated and gay, and reminds my father why he chose her all those years ago. I make myself talk to him, asking about his latest job prospects and where we'll be moving next, and, for once, dredge up the charm I inherited from him.

Finally, mellowed by bourbon and wine and good food and my mother's attention, he asks, "What is all this for? I haven't been your favorite person for a long time, DG. What are you two up to?"

My mother laughs and tells him, "We have a surprise for you. Something we've been planning for a while. You are going to love it."

He arches a brow, looking at us skeptically. "What is this going to cost me?"

My mother laughs again and waves away his concerns. "Almost nothing! And she doesn't have to go far away, either. Look."

I sit paralyzed while my mother lays bare our deception. She has decided to play this like a scene from a Noel Coward play. She spins an amusing tale of little lies and little economies, and takes as much of the credit and blame as she can for herself.

"It was all my idea," she tells him. "I knew you didn't want her to go far away, so this is what I came up with. I had to force her to do it, and to keep it a secret."

She flashes my transcripts at him, knowing that he likely won't understand them. My father's lack of education is his secret shame. He hides it whenever possible. "So, you've been lying to me all this time." This is the response I fear.

My mother perches on the arm of his chair. She leans over him, adding her heady perfume to that of the bourbon and the wine. "Don't be silly! It wasn't a bad lie. Just a way to help you see what might happen. DG doesn't have to go so far away. She can meet a perfectly nice young man in Austin, just three hours away—two, the way you drive! And the cost is nothing compared to sending her to live in Europe."

I'm afraid she's overplaying it. She's too flighty, too careless about everything. As if my life doesn't depend on his response.

"DG, what do you have to say for yourself?" His voice is harsh. My mother stiffens. I've said nothing so far, trying to stay out of it, trying not to want.

"It's a good idea, Daddy." I try not choke on the word. "I would like to try." My voice is small and flat.

He watches me closely, then demands, "Explain all this paperwork."

I open the envelope and smooth the folded papers flat. "These papers show my grades for the classes I've already taken. I used them to apply to UT in Austin, because it is close." I explain that my grades are very good, and that I even have a part in a play on campus next week. He can come and see me in it, if he's in town and if he wants to. "I would like you to be there," I lie.

"You don't think you want to be an actress, showing your-self off, do you?" he demands.

"No, sir," I respond. "This is just for fun, nothing serious. I want to study English, maybe be a teacher." Another lie. I have no idea what I want to be, but a teacher is respectable, he'll like that. He grunts, and I keep explaining papers to him.

"These are for housing. I want to live in a girls' dorm," I tell him. Still another lie. I don't care where I live. I just want out of here.

My mother and I go through the papers, explaining the costs, and she stresses again how cheap it is to send me to Austin. He asks an occasional question, and keeps a close eye on both of us. I feel as if I am tightrope-walking without a net.

When we are done, my mother pours him one more bour-bon, and we wait. He sips several times, and tells us, "I'll have to think about it." He rises from the table, takes my mother's hand, and leads her away. She looks back over her shoulder just once, then leans into his arm. I can hear her voice, but not what she says as they leave the dining room.

I am left with the ruins of dinner and the beginnings of hope.

Darling Girl was typeset in Minion. In designing Minion font, Robert Slimbach was inspired by the timeless beauty of the fonts of the late Renaissance. Minion was created primarily as a traditional text font but adapts well to today's digital technology, presenting the richness of the late baroque forms within modern text formats. This clear, balanced font is suitable for almost any use. The name comes from the traditional naming system for type sizes, in which minion is between nonpareil and brevier, with the type body 7pt in height. As the name suggests, it is particularly intended as a font for body text in a classical style, neutral and practical while also slightly condensed to save space. Slimbach described the design as having "a simplified structure and moderate proportions." The ornaments, or dingbats, used throughout the text are also from the Minion family.

∾

DESIGN BY DEDE CUMMINGS
BRATTLEBORO, VERMONT

CPSIA information can be obtained
at www.ICGtesting.com
Printed in the USA
LVHW03s1359300818
588449LV00006B/6/P